Bobbie Mendoza Saves the World (Again*)

Bobbie Mendoza Saves the World (Again)

Written by Michael Fry and Bradley Jackson

Illustrated by Michael Fry

HARPER

An Imprint of HarperCollinsPublishers

Library of Congress Cataloging-in-Publication Data

Names: Fry, Michael, author, illustrator. | Jackson, Bradley, author.
Title: Bobbie Mendoza saves the world (again) / written by Michael Fry and Bradley
    Jackson ; illustrated by Michael Fry.
Description: First edition. | New York, NY : Harper, an imprint of HarperCollinsPublishers,
    [2018] | Sequel to: The naughty list. | Summary: Twelve-year-old Bobbie wants to fit
    in at her new school, but an obnoxious classmate, a bounty hunter, and two elves
    asking for her help are there at every turn.
Identifiers: LCCN 2018004915 | ISBN 978-0-06-265193-8 (hardback)
Subjects: | CYAC: Imaginary creatures--Fiction. | Bounty hunters--Fiction. | Middle
    schools--Fiction. | Schools--Fiction. | Humorous stories. | BISAC: JUVENILE
    FICTION / Humorous Stories. | JUVENILE FICTION / Fantasy & Magic. |
    JUVENILE FICTION / Social Issues / Self-Esteem & Self-Reliance.
Classification: LCC PZ7.F9234 Bm 2018 | DDC [Fic]--dc23 LC record available at https://
    lccn.loc.gov/2018004915

Typography by Celeste Knudsen
18 19 20 21 22   CG/LSCH   10 9 8 7 6 5 4 3 2 1
❖

First Edition

To Neva, a true patron of the arts.—M.F.

To Mom and Dad—thanks for making me, *me*. And for a
whole bunch of other stuff too. I love you tons.—B.J.

Foreword

Being special is a *nightmare*.

It's true. I know these things. How?

Because *I'm* special.

Don't believe me? I'll prove it to you.

You know that Christmas that almost never happened? Wait. You don't remember? What do you mean you don't remember? Oh, that's right, you don't remember that Christmas that almost never happened because . . .

Yeah, that's right. Me. Bobbie Mendoza. Age twelve. Christmas saver kid-person.

But before that I was a mostly normal tween-age girl. (Note: please forget I used the word "tween-age.")

I liked normal stuff: like painting my little brother Tad's toenails black with yellow stars when he's asleep. Or convincing my mom that waffle-pops are part of a nutritious breakfast, lunch, and dinner. Or helping my dad dress up our dog, Maggie, to look like a hipster.

FEDORA

HIPSTER BEARD

WOVEN BRACELETS

Yup, then I became the "chosen one." Chosen by two elves (yeah, elves, you heard me) to travel to the North Pole by whale (that's right, a whale) and fight off demon snow angels and this creepy/scary Watcher machine in order to save Christmas. (I'm not making this up.)

I'm sure you read all about it. Except you didn't. And THAT'S why being special . . .

I thought when I got back from saving Christmas that maybe I'd be given a medal or a ribbon or at least a participation trophy.

It wasn't like I was expecting a parade in my honor or raspberry waffle-pops with the president or a personalized romantic ballad sung by my favorite singer,

Jonas Jerklin. (No! I don't think he's dreamy. He just sings really, really well.)

Did I just swoon out loud?

But of course none of that happened. And that's what they don't teach you in Being Special 101. When you get back from your magical adventure, where you have to be brave and overcome impossible odds and discover who you really are . . . there's just one tiny little problem.

NO ONE KNOWS ABOUT IT!

Because . . .

Mostly because no one would believe it. But also because . . . where would I begin?

So I figured if I can't tell anyone about it, then it might be best to pretend it never happened, right? If I can't stand out, might as well blend in! There was only one problem with that. This guy.

He's my uncle Dale. And he's weird. Not weird-uncle weird. We're talking texts-with-elves weird. And this was before I saved Christmas. Back when he used to rant about Trans-Dimensional Barriers and cheer power, and we all thought he was crazy. But then I saved Christmas and it all turned out . . .

He's so happy now that he knows he's not crazy that he doesn't understand why I'm not happy. He doesn't get that not being able to tell my crazy story is a real bummer.

Especially since I'm about to start at a brand-new school tomorrow. I know I'm supposed to be this battle-hardened Christmas-saving warrior, but the thought of having to fit in and make a whole set of new friends is causing me to FREAK OUT!

What if I can't relate to them? What if they think I'm super weird?! What if I blurt out some crazy factoid about reindeer bladder leakage in the middle of lunch?

Fortunately, Uncle Dale tried to help.

He found me a place where I can tell my story. He found a support group for folks who have encountered Trans-Dimensional Beings.

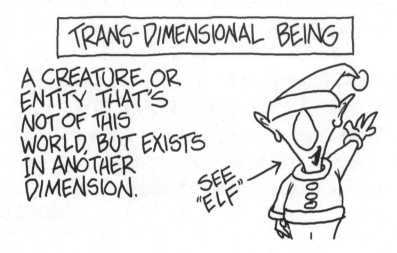

TRANS-DIMENSIONAL BEING

A CREATURE OR ENTITY THAT'S NOT OF THIS WORLD, BUT EXISTS IN ANOTHER DIMENSION.

SEE "ELF"

A Trans-Dimensional Being is, generally speaking, something or someone that if you're seeing it you probably shouldn't be. It's weird. It's strange. But it's NOT like my neighbor Mr. Billups, who mixes tuna salad with ketchup and anchovies.

Uncle Dale thought I needed some like-minded people to share my feelings. The problem is, these people are just as crazy as he is!

Trust me, nothing makes you want to be normal more than sitting around a group of people who swear a werewolf once delivered them Chinese food or how they saw a mer-man riding around on a Segway.

So that's where I am right now. Trying to be normal. AT THE LEAST NORMAL-EST PLACE ON EARTH!

Help!

Chapter 1

So this is how I spent my Sunday evenings—in the smelly old gymnasium of the Nondenominational Church of Happiness and Stuff with my uncle Dale and fourteen other poor souls who claimed to have had an encounter with a Trans-Dimensional Being.

How was this going to help me at school tomorrow?

"Thank you, Ms. Ginsburg," said the group leader, Topher.

Topher is deadly boring. His only claim to TDB fame was growing up next door to a Sasquatch (who may or may not have just been some really hairy dude).

HAIRY DUDE

SASQUATCH

BIG FOOT

ANOTHER BIG FOOT

HUG ME I'M HAIRY

Topher turned his attention to me. "Bobbie, do you have anything to share?"

Of course I didn't have anything to share.

But if you don't share, if you say, "Nah, I'm fine, Toph, I'm just here for the stale donuts," then he just keeps poking and prodding you until you lose your temper or share everything in one long emotional rant. Sort of like a mom.

Normally I'd cave, but I've got a system. Watch and learn.

Aren't I clever?

"Guess that means it's my turn!" boomed Uncle Dale.

Uncle Dale loves it when it's his turn. He doesn't have any trouble sharing. Especially on his website.

Since that Christmas thing I mentioned, traffic to his site has nearly tripled. From twelve monthly visitors to thirty-five.

Uncle Dale is weird, but it's a good kind of weird. The kind that takes the attention off me.

Most of the time.

Uncle Dale addressed the group. "Bobbie starts a new school tomorrow and she's terrified of not being able to relate to anyone or make any new friends because they may find out what happened to her in

4

the Trans-Dimensional World."

Wait. What?

Every eye turned to me.

Topher smiled. "Well, Bobbie, it does seem like you have more to share."

I sighed. "Are you sure we can't go back to Ms. Ginsburg and her farting chimney pterodactyl?"

Uncle Dale put his hand on my shoulder. "It's okay, Bobbie, we're here to help."

I'd had enough.

"Fine!" I shouted. "I don't want the new kids at my school to think I'm weird. I don't want to accidentally talk about how I know Santa or I've seen things that everyone else would think are crazy BUT I KNOW are real! I want to fit in! I want to forget what I saw! I want to forget what I did!"

Great. Now the rest of the session was going to be about me, my problems, and ME! I needed a distraction. I needed someone to save me. I needed a miracle!

Be careful what you wish for.

Chapter 2

The scary Amazon Viking lady was in my face with all the confidence and poise of an exploding can of Cheez Whiz.

Topher rushed to his feet. "Excuse me, but this is a private meeting!"

The Viking gal grabbed Topher by his bow tie. "Private?! Listen up, Soft-Spot. Ain't nothing gonna be private when vampires and trolls and zombie squid are running wild in the streets. I'm talking chaos, people. Mass hysteria!"

She marched around the room and glared at each

of us in turn. Then she grabbed one of Dale's donuts, shoved it in her mouth, and sat down. Right next to me. No one said a word.

Next time I wish for a miracle I'll be more specific.

She leaned over and smiled at me. "So you want to pretend like it never happened! Lemme tell you something, little miss missy, an attitude like that is gonna get you roasted, toasted, and swallowed whole by a dragon-bear."

A what?

"You got any idea what that is?!" she shouted.

I cleared my throat. "I assume it's a creature that's part dragon and part bear?"

She paused for a brief moment. "Good guess."

Then she turned to the others. "As for the rest of you! With your whiny, crybaby stories of 'Oh . . . wha wha, Elvis is my Uber driver, whaaa. I got two words for ya . . ."

Topher—sounding like a mouse whispering into a cave—attempted to speak. "Ma'am, we understand you're upset, but if you could please let us finish our meeting and then perhaps you and I could talk . . . in private, away from everyone else."

The crazy lady started laughing. Not a "that's-so-funny" kind of laugh. No, it was the kind of laugh you hear in old movies when the villain has the good guy hanging over a tank of hungry beavers and he thinks it's over, but it's not over because the good guy can speak telepathically with the beavers and tells them to eat the villain. But what the good guy *doesn't* know is that the villain holds all the beavers' children hostage until they eat the good guy.

Topher gulped as Laughing Lady walked toward him. We all watched it unfold like a beautiful slow-motion train wreck.

"I don't understand what's so funny," said Topher.

"Sure you don't . . . But maybe you'll start laughing if I tickle your gigantic feet!"

"BIGFOOT!" shouted Uncle Dale with glee.

The rest of us just stared, openmouthed. Great. This is exactly the type of thing I was hoping to not see before my first day of school tomorrow.

"That's right," said Loraine, "all this time your little support group has been led by a Class B Metatarsus Abnormality with Extreme Filamental Outgrowth!"

"Bigfoot." Uncle Dale nodded.

I mean sure, we've all seen the blurry pictures, but none of them looked as terrified as Topher did. I felt sorry for him as the scary lady dragged him toward the door.

I looked at Uncle Dale. "Who in the heck was that?!" I asked.

"Loraine. Loraine the Bounty Hunter. And we need to talk to her!"

Chapter 3

We caught up to Loraine as she started to get into her ancient VW Bug.

Uncle Dale cried, "Loraine! Loraine! Hold up a sec!"

Loraine turned to Uncle Dale. "Who are you?"

"Sorry," said Uncle Dale. "I'm Dale Mendoza and this is my niece, Bobbie. We're both huge fans."

"What?" I said.

Uncle Dale continued, "That were-zombie you captured in Portland last week was a thing of beauty!"

"You know about that?" Loraine said.

"Of course I know . . . you may read my blog . . . theyreeverywhere.com."

"Hmmmm . . . You wrote that story about the recent unicorn influx."

"That was me!" said Dale proudly.

She looked Dale over. "You got some stuff wrong. Unicorns don't poop glitter—they poop rainbows. And did you know their horns are poisonous?"

I rolled my eyes and laughed. "Poisonous unicorn horns? Right."

"Laugh if you want, little lady," said Loraine. "Those horns emit a slumberification toxin that puts whoever they sting into a fifteen- to twenty-minute coma."

"Sounds like a nap," I said.

"The victims do seem to wake up relaxed and refreshed," said Loraine.

I nodded. "A nap."

Uncle Dale started taking notes. "And the rest of my article?" he asked.

Loraine turned back to her car. "The rest of it was okay."

Uncle Dale swooned. "Thhhhankyou! You have no idea how much that means to me! Would you be willing to write a guest column?!"

I'd had enough.

"What'd you do with Bigfoot Topher?" I demanded.

Loraine held up a small necklace. "I used a non-particle destabilization shrink-ifier."

HE'S IN HERE WITH A FEW OF MY OTHER PRIZE CATCHES.

"But of course," I said. "A non-particle destabilization SHRINK-IFIER. Does that come with Wi-Fi?!"

Loraine smiled. "You bet. And the password is UR_NOT_FUNNY . . . all uppercase."

I am too funny. Everyone says so.

Uncle Dale tried to ease the tension. "How exactly did Topher camouflage himself like a Bigfoot?"

Loraine shook her head. "There's an app for that."

Dale inspected the app. "So a Glargantasaur can turn itself into a sixty-six-year-old grandmother of seven from Des Moines named Janice?"

Loraine nodded. "Don't you love technology?"

"You must be working for SCUD," said Dale.

"Freelance. Bounty hunting is the game. Loraine is the name."

"SCUD?" I asked.

Loraine sighed. "The Security Council of United Dimensions."

"It's an organization of Inter-Dimensional and Trans-Dimensional Beings who work together to maintain the Trans-Dimensional Boundary," explained Dale.

"And we're seeing a lot of activity this side of the boundary. It's never been worse. Not sure what's going on, but something's got 'em jumping. That's why SCUD has assembled my NICE List."

"Huh?" I said.

Nasty Imaginary Creatures Escaping

Dale lit up. "Can Bobbie and I help?!"

Loraine glared at us. "I work alone."

Good for her. I admire independent, strong women.

She turned, slid into her clown car, and drove off into the night.

Uncle Dale smiled. "Alone? We'll see about that."

Chapter 4

So instead of having a nice, relaxing night before my first day of school, I had to watch our tiny group leader get turned into a Bigfoot and endure a Trans-Dimensional lecture from an angry bounty hunter telling me all about how I need to watch out for were-zombies and unicorn poop.

I was on edge.

My mom and dad could tell.

Mom fake-smiled. "You're going to do great tomorrow at your new school!"

Dad matched Mom's fake smile. "Just a suggestion

but I'm thinking if you wear something other than black it might go better for you."

As I've said before, black goes with everything.

Even me.

Mom's smile grew. "Yeah! And maybe smile at people! Or a person. One person. Or the floor. You decide."

What?

Yeah. That's going to help.

Dad's smile started to fade. "You're going to do great, kiddo, just great!"

Great. Just great.

I went up to my room and lay down. As I stared at the ceiling, I tried this old trick I do that usually calms me down. I made a list of all the bad things that could happen. I know it sounds crazy, but once I make a list

and read it out loud, I realize how crazy it all sounds.
It works.

BOBBIE'S FIRST-DAY-OF-NEW-SCHOOL NIGHTMARES

1. PANTS CATCH FIRE.
2. SNORT CORN OUT MY NOSE AT LUNCH.
3. SAY "IN DA FUZZY MOLE" INSTEAD OF "INDIVISIBLE" DURING PLEDGE OF ALLEGIANCE.
4. RUN WITH SCISSORS. FALL. STAB GYM TEACHER.
5. GET ASKED WHAT I DID OVER CHRISTMAS VACATION.

Most of the time. But not tonight.

Calm down, Bobbie. Deep breaths. In one, two, three. Out one, two, three.

One. Two. Three.

One.

Two.

Zzzzzzzzzzzzz.

Chapter 5

I'm asleep. I think. I'm not sure. It's not like when you're asleep you can tell if you're asleep. If you think about it, you can't even tell when you're awake if you're asleep. I mean, maybe we're always asleep and when we wake up we just wake up in another dream that *seems* like we're awake. We're *always* asleep. Asleep on some alien dream farm where they grow bodies for spare parts. And the alien doctors argue about what to harvest first.

Wait. What was that? Out of the corner of my eye. Something moved. Something big. It went behind that huge cactus with the laughing cow heads.

I'm dreaming. I'm sure of it. But it's not the laughing cow head cactus that tipped me off. Who hasn't seen a laughing cow head cactus before?

Suddenly, there it was again. Out of the corner of my eye. I turn, but it's gone . . . right behind the giant toilet paper roll.

I sneak up to the roll and peek behind it. Nothing. Well, nothing except a green lake of lime Jell-O and a large spork. Hmm . . . don't mind if I do.

Some people dream in color. Me? I dream in flavors. Mostly lime. But sometimes cherry and grape. Never licorice.

Just as I was about to dive in for another bite a cute little wormy thing popped out of the Jell-O. It wiggled hello at me.

How cute. Then another one popped up. And another. And another. My, that's a lot of wormy things wiggling hello, I thought. That's when I noticed the suction cups on the wormy things. And I realized they weren't wormy things.

THEY'RE TENTACLES!

And they were after me!

I froze. That's when the tentacles wrapped around me in a death grip. The Jell-O started to boil and I came face-to-face with . . .

HOO-BOY!

A part of me was terrified, sure. But another part was like, this is weird. Still another part was, hey, this is all dream. But then the last part said . . .

The giant squid opened its mouth revealing rows of razor-sharp teeth. I was done for. It was going to eat me. But I didn't scream. I didn't cry out. I just wondered . . .

That's when I woke up. And that's when I said,

After I stopped feeling my heartbeat in my eyelids, I figured the giant squid nightmare must have something to do with going to the new school. My mind was just playing tricks on me! There is no giant squid.

Breathe. One. Two. Three. Calm. Down.

It's just a new school. It's nothing to be afraid of.

Breathe. One. Two. Three.

Because I would do more than just "fit in." I would be invisible. I would fly so far "under the radar" that no one would even know I was there!

I would go full stealth, middle-school ninja.

I mean, fitting in is easier if no one even knows you're there, right?

Yeah. That didn't happen. This happened.

So much for blending in.

Chapter 6

There's this thing my dad says when I'm giving every-body the silent treatment.

WHAT'S THE MATTER, KIDDO?
CAT GOT YOUR TONGUE?

MEAT CAKE

Like a lot things my dad says . . .

. . . it doesn't make much sense.

The cat thing didn't make any sense either until one day we were cat-sitting Mr. Gibbles from next door and I made the mistake of falling asleep on our couch.

I coughed up cat fur for the next three days every time I tried to speak.

Which is exactly how I felt when twenty-two strange kids at St. Regents Prep stared at me as I attempted to "tell them about myself."

The teacher saw the terror in my eyes.

"Bobbie? Christmas holidays?"

Oh yeah. That.

"Okay, thank you, Bobbie," said the teacher. "We're glad you're here."

I slid back into my seat and let out a sigh of relief. I'd survived my worst nightmare. Everybody bought it! I could officially start my life over as a regular old twelve-year-old!

Hang on.

Chapter 7

The kid's name was Cole Crusterman. He wasn't like the other kids. He wasn't like *any* kid. He had a LOT of extra-curricular activities.

BUSINESS SCROLL

EDITOR OF SCHOOL NEWSPAPER. PRESIDENT OF THE SCRAPBOOKING CLUB. CAPTAIN OF THE SYNCHRONIZED ORIGAMI TEAM... BLAH, BLAH, BLAH...

To say this kid was an overachiever was an understatement.

The bell rang. I darted out of class as fast as I could. But not fast enough to escape Cole.

"Wait up!" he shouted after me. "I was hoping I could interview you?"

"For what?"

"A profile piece for the school paper," he said. "My profiles are super popular, second only to my eight-part cafeteria exposé. . . ."

No way was this happening. But before I could get in his face he held out his phone to record me and continued.

"Smile, you're being live-streamed," said Cole.

"Live-streamed?" I asked. "Who the heck would be watching that?"

"Currently no one, but I'm hopeful for my first viewer soon!"

This kid's nuts.

"So I was on your uncle's site," he continued. "Very interesting. Do you share any of your uncle's interests?"

I yelled, "NO! Uncle Dale and I have NOTHING in common!"

"What about Phil and Dew Drop?"

"Gumdrop."

Cole stared at me.

I stammered, "I . . . I . . . I don't know why I said that. I don't know any Phil or Gumdrop or any elves for that matter!"

Cole smiled. "Who said anything about elves?"

This kid was really getting on my nerves. I grabbed his phone and said,

UNCLE DALE IS CRAZY!

Cole said, "Is that on the record?"

We arrived at my locker.

"No!" I said. "I mean, yes. I mean . . . I don't know what I mean. Please, just leave me alone. I'm just a supernormal kid. Believe me. Totally normal. Nothing weird about me. No, sirree. BORING!"

I opened my locker.

Chapter 8

I slammed my locker shut.

"You okay?" asked Cole.

This was a must-lie situation.

"Uhhhh . . . it's a spider. A huge, hairy . . . farting spider."

"Whoa! Really? Lucky for you I'm head of the school's Arachnids Are Awesome Association. I'd love to photograph it for our blog!"

What is wrong with this kid?

Okay, so I'm not proud about this next part, but something drastic had to be done.

I slammed my locker shut. "You're really nosy. I want you to mind your own business and leave me alone. I'm not talking to you or your stupid newspaper or your live stream that nobody watches!"

Cole looked hurt.

He looked down at his shoes. "Thank you for your time, Bobbie. I hope you'll reconsider."

He left. I felt bad. But I had no choice, right? I had two diminutive sprite beings in my locker. At least they were being quiet.

Chapter 9

Ugh . . . elves.

Other than being super annoyed, the first thing I noticed was that they weren't exactly dressed how I remembered.

IN-SEASON ELVES

OFF-SEASON ELVES
← FEZZES
THONGS

"Wait, what's with the weird hats?" I asked.

Phil sighed. "It's a fez. It's hip. It's happening. It's today!"

"It hides my bald spot," added Gumdrop.

I said, "And the skimpy bathing suits?"

"If you must know," said Gumdrop, "we've been lifeguards in the Bermuda Triangle for the last fifty off-seasons."

"Off-season?" I said.

"North Pole work is seasonal," said Phil. "Once the holidays are over we gotta look for other work in the Trans-Dimensional World."

"No way," I said.

"Way," said Phil. "Serious freaky way."

HEY, GODZILLA! OUT OF THE WAVE POOL!

Enough of this nonsense. "What are you doing in my locker?" I demanded.

"We need your help, Bobbie," said Phil.

"Yes, we are in a most precarious situation," Gumdrop added. "It would seem the Trans-Dimensional Barrier that separates our two worlds is experiencing a bit of a hiccup."

"It's crumbling faster than a decade-old donut," added Phil.

"And that's led to a rather large influx of creatures crossing the boundary," said Gumdrop.

I've heard this story before.

"What does any of this have to do with me?" I asked.

"We need your cheer, Bobbie!" said Gumdrop.

"Big-time," said Phil.

I'd had enough.

"Oh, so I assume you want me to just cross over into your Bizarro-Narnia again and almost die again and then I'll just come back even weirder and crazier than I was before, AGAIN! Is that what you want?" I asked.

Phil and Gumdrop grinned. "Yes!"

RINNNG!!

The bell. Great. Now I was late to my next class.
I looked back at Phil and Gumdrop and shook my
head.

Chapter 10

I made it to class.

After the bell.

"Ah, you must be Roberta Mendoza. So nice of you to join us," said my science teacher, Mr. Lindenberger. "Are you going to make a habit of being late?"

As the students stared I contemplated telling him the truth.

Bad idea. Instead I just mumbled an apology into the floor and hoped for the best.

I've got to stop hoping.

"Sorry, sir, she's late because of me!" a familiar voice shouted from the front of the room.

It was Cole. Again. He was stalking me!

"She was giving me an exclusive interview for the paper and I guess we just lost track of time. Apologies, sir."

"Very well, then, Roberta . . . since you're already so chummy with Mr. Crusterman, you can join him as a lab partner for today's lesson."

Perfect. Just perfect, I thought. My day just kept getting better and better.

I sat next to Cole as Mr. Lindenberger began walking us through the boring safety regulations of the science lab. You know the usual science class rules . . .

"You're welcome," Cole whispered.

"Listen, Cole," I said. "I don't know who you think you are, but—"

I looked up. Mr. Lindenberger was glaring down at me. "Ms. Mendoza, are you trying to stand out as a chatterbox on your first day of school?"

"No, sir," I mumbled.

As Mr. Lindenberger went back to explaining how not to blow ourselves up, I decided the best way to handle Cole was to IGNORE HIM.

There's a word I learned at my old school that I really liked: "OBLIVIOUS." It means not aware or not concerned by what's going on around you.

That would be me. I would become CAPTAIN OBLIVIOUS!

Mr. Lindenberger said, "Reach into the cabinets at your stations and take out your Bunsen burners, please."

Captain Oblivious versus Team Obnoxious.

Chapter 11

"Another problem, Roberta?" asked Mr. Lindenberger.

"No, sir! No problem. Just not sure which Bunsen burner to pick! They're all so great!"

He rolled his eyes. "Cole, please fetch a Bunsen burner for your lab partner."

They're still here! I thought. How am I going to get out of this?

Mr. Lindenberger continued, "The Bunsen burner produces an open gas flame, which is used for heating, sterilization, and combustion."

From above, Phil muttered, "I'll show him a gas combustion!"

"Why are you two following me?" I whispered under my breath.

Cole whispered, "Who are you talking to?"

"No one! Don't look up—" But Cole was already looking up.

Nothing. They'd disappeared again. Or maybe I was seeing things? Was I crazy? Is there a medical condition for seeing imaginary elves on your first day of school? Was I one step away from being locked in a special facility for troubled tweens?

"PSST! In here!" said Gumdrop's voice from inside my backpack.

Nope. I wasn't crazy.

As Cole followed our teacher's instructions and lit the Bunsen burner, I quietly peered inside my backpack.

Mr. Lindenberger raised his voice. "Ms. Mendoza! No cell phones inside my class. Hand it over this instant!"

He was across the room, a lit Bunsen burner in one hand, and his other hand outstretched.

Everyone in our class *ooooh*ed like I was in serious trouble.

The problem was I didn't have a cell phone in my backpack.

"Hand it over!"

I guess I waited too long because in the blink of an eye he'd put his Bunsen burner down and was at my side, dumping the contents of my backpack onto my desk.

I waited for Phil and Gumdrop to tumble out and for the local mental hospital to be called to take me away for good. But nothing happened.

Just my brand-new textbooks, a binder, and half a dozen pens and pencils tumbled out.

Mr. Lindenberger stared at me. "Hand over the cell phone now or it's morning detention for you!"

There was literally no way this day could get any worse.

That's when I saw Phil—back on the ceiling—he

had a lit Bunsen burner and a mischievous look in his eye.

Nope. It can always get worse.

Chapter 12

Morning detention. That was my punishment.

Texting/tweeting in class was my crime. The fact that I had no phone didn't seem to be important.

I confessed instantly because it's a lot better than telling the truth: that I was fending off two fart-flaming elves from luring me on yet another Trans-Dimensional adventure.

That night I went home, and Mom and Dad were understandably concerned, but they knew to give me my space. Uncle Dale seemed unusually quiet too.

Either way, I was glad because I wasn't in the mood to talk to anyone.

After dinner I lay on my bed feeling frustrated that no matter how hard I tried to fit in, I just seemed to stand out more.

Huh? Was Uncle Dale playing a prank on me?

"Is someone there?" I asked, but my voice just echoed like I was inside a racquetball court.

Suddenly I couldn't move. And then it came for me again.

I jolted awake as sweat dripped down my forehead. It took me a while to catch my breath. I'd had bad dreams before, but never the same one twice in a row.

Was something wrong with me? Was I doomed to never fit in anywhere because of all that I'd seen? Would I ever be able to eat calamari again?

I didn't have time to think about it because my first ever morning detention was right around the corner. Hopefully, the day wouldn't be worse than yesterday, right?

Chapter 13

Morning detention wasn't as bad as everyone made it out to be. It was quiet, no one in the hallways or classrooms. And the person watching me was the assistant gym coach, Mr. Rasmussen, who fell asleep five minutes into the session.

The only problem was I sensed Phil and Gumdrop were still stalking me (everything smelled vaguely of cinnamon). Also, Uncle Dale seemed to be texting a lot before he dropped me off at detention this morning. Something felt weird. . . .

But I was determined to make this day into a normal day. That is until . . .

Why on earth was this kid here this early dressed like a unicorn?!

"I get here early for mascot practice. Big pep rally this afternoon. The whole school's going to be there!" said Cole, now the unicorn.

I said, "Don't let me stop you."

"I just wanted to see if you were okay. That was strange what happened yesterday in science class."

"I'm fine."

"Who were you talking to?" he asked.

"No one!"

"Was it Phil and Gumball?"

"Gumdrop . . . never mind! You're kind of nosy, you know that?" I said.

"Well, you're kind of weird, you know that?" he said.

"This from the kid who gets to school early wearing a unicorn costume?!"

"Hey, there's nothing wrong with being weird. Weird is interesting. Weird is different. Weird is your story."

"Well, I guess this is the end of my story, because other than a strange kid bothering me in a unicorn costume—nothing weird happens to me!"

That's when a giant net suddenly wrapped him up and I heard a familiar voice nearly drowned out by two high-pitched squeals.

Chapter 14

Can't a girl just get through one detention without a trigger-happy Trans-Dimensional bounty hunter busting in with two annoying elves already tied up in her net? I looked up at Loraine. She looked determined. Like a dog with a bone—a *T-rex* leg bone that was too big for her mouth. It fit, but only because she could unhinge her jaws like a python. A weird Viking she-python. Where was I?

"What are you doing here?!" I shouted.

"My job!" announced Loraine.

LONG LINE

CARTOONIST

LORAINE

I must have missed that line at the job fair.

"Help, help, help!" shouted Cole.

"My goodness," said Loraine. "This unicorn can talk!"

I said, "That's because it's not a real unicorn; it's a kid in a unicorn costume!"

"That's weird," said Loraine.

Seriously? This was the weird part? Whatever.

This was not how I wanted my first detention to go. I needed to get Cole out of that net and get Loraine and Phil and Gumdrop out of there before Mr. Rasmussen woke up.

Cole ripped his unicorn head off, saw Phil and Gumdrop tied up, and cried out, "It's true! It's all true!" he said.

Loraine cut him free from the net. "Now excuse me while I transport these two tiny TDBs back across the border for processing. Next time you see anything else weird or strange, stay outta my way."

Cole's eyes widened and his mouth dropped as he pointed just behind Loraine.

". . . Like th . . . th . . . that?" he mumbled.

"Like what?" asked Loraine as she turned around.

Chapter 15

Here's the thing they don't tell you about real uni-corns. They smell. And not like rainbows or lavender or sugarplum daffodils, but more like an actual horse that's been bathing exclusively in some weird combi-nation of maple syrup and gym socks.

I think I was in shock. Which is what happens when you're trapped in the principal's office on your sec-ond day of school with a Trans-Dimensional bounty hunter, two annoying elves, your bizarro uncle, and the never-ending question machine that is Cole Crus-terman.

Oh, and the unicorn(s). Plural.

"Shhhh . . . No one move a muscle," warned Loraine. "This is by far the largest unicorn infestation I've seen since . . ."

"The Boca Raton incident of '03," Uncle Dale said.

You could tell Dale hoped Loraine would be impressed with his knowledge, but she talked over him. "The only way this many could possibly cross onto the other side of the realm is if . . ."

She glared down toward Gumdrop and Phil.

"Shut up and stay here," Loraine barked. "These things might look cute and cuddly, but they're wild creatures. They'll sting you to sleep faster than you can say holy hippogriff."

Lame. I can say "holy hippogriff" pretty darn fast.

Loraine pulled out two long sticks with prods at the end that hummed with what sounded like weird, twinkling electricity. Uncle Dale's eyes widened.

"Is that a Uni-Prod?" he asked.

"Yeah, too many for nets. I can herd them back into the portal with these babies."

"Be careful," said Uncle Dale with a bit too much real concern. "All those horns could sting you to sleep for eight to ten hours."

That sounds nice.

"Careful is for cowards!" snorted Loraine as she dumped Phil and Gumdrop out on the floor and set out after the unicorns.

Uncle Dale helped the elves to their feet. "Thanks for the heads-up, guys. Is the hot-air balloon gassed and ready to go?"

Wait a minute. Hot-air balloon? Uncle Dale is in on this. Again!

"But Bobbie won't go with us," said Phil.

Uncle Dale shot me a look. "C'mon, Bobbie! Phil and Gumdrop need our help!"

I said, "How many ways do I have say this to make this clear? I'VE QUIT THE BEING-SPECIAL BUSINESS!"

"No time to argue," said Uncle Dale. "With Loraine distracted, we've only got a brief window."

Phil pointed at Cole. "What about the kid?"

Cole was in shock. He just kept repeating, "Unicorns. In the hallway. Unicorns. In the hallway."

I felt sorry for Cole because now he was just like me. He'd seen something so unbelievable he couldn't write a story about it because everyone would think he was crazy too.

Been there. Hated that.

I wanted to give him a pat on the back and tell him it would be all right, but c'mon, who am I kidding? It's never going to be all right. It's just going to be weird. At least until you forgot about it. Which was still my plan right up until Uncle Dale grabbed me and pointed down the hall.

Chapter 16

Have you ever seen a unicorn stampede?

It's equal amounts adorable and bizarre. And a lot more rainbow poop than you'd imagine.

Colorful poop aside, here I was being chased and dragged—no, FORCED—into ANOTHER insane

Trans-Dimensional freakathon as we headed straight for my locker!

Phil hurled the door open. My books and binders were gone, replaced by a . . . wait. What?

Behind me Loraine yelled, "Oh no you don't! Stop right there!"

Gumdrop and Phil jumped through the portal. They beckoned me to follow.

And that was the exact moment when Cole Crusterman volunteered as a crazy person.

Uncle Dale looked at me, then back at Loraine and the charging unicorns. He gave me a sad look. "C'mon, Bobbie, we need you."

"No. You don't!"

Uncle Dale gave me his best "I'm disappointed in you" look, then jumped into the locker.

"Comin' through!" yelled Loraine.

Before I could say anything, the unicorns were on me and I had to duck.

Loraine ran up and stopped before following. "You made the right choice, kid. Those fools are getting locked away for a long time."

Wait, what?! Locked away? What did that mean?

I watched as Loraine pulled out a crazy-looking weapon, aimed it through my locker, and fired.

I couldn't believe it. Were Uncle Dale, Phil, Gumdrop, and Cole really going to be locked away by Loraine? Did I abandon them? Did they really need me like Uncle Dale said?

Just then the fun-sized unicorn nuzzled up against me. I guess she'd somehow escaped Loraine's grasp.

That's when I had a crazy idea.

So much for morning detention. Or school. Or the whole not-being-special thing.

Chapter 17

I rode Señorita Sparkles through my magical portal/locker and into another dimension. Yeah. I named her. I was in a hurry. Don't judge.

I had a plan. No, not a plan. More like an idea. Well, not an idea exactly. More like a . . . Okay, I had no clue what I was going to do.

As we galloped through the grassy meadow, I saw Loraine securing a large net containing Uncle Dale, Cole, Phil, and Gumdrop.

I rode closer and closer. Señorita Sparkles lowered her head, leading with her horn. That's when I figured out what I was going to do. Or Sparkles figured it out for me.

Loraine was out like a light.

I guess it was pretty awesome. I tried to hide my smile as I untied them from the net.

Once freed, they all ran toward the hot-air balloon.

Uncle Dale beckoned me. "C'mon, Bobbie!"

"No way," I said. "I'm going back to class."

That's when Uncle Dale pointed behind me.

I glanced over my shoulder and saw Loraine slowly trying to get up from her brief unicorn slumber.

She jumped for me. I ran.

"Hurry! Faster!" shouted Phil.

I dove into the balloon's basket. Gumdrop made quick work of the rope and we slowly began to ascend. Loraine dove . . .

. . . and missed.

Loraine shook her fist at us and screamed, "I'll get you! Just you wait! I'll hunt you down! You can't escape Loraine the Bounty Hunter!"

Chapter 18

It was all a bad dream.

It had to be.

Who jumps through a locker into another dimension and then boards a hot-air balloon after being chased by a Trans-Dimensional bounty hunter?

Crazy people.

I am not a crazy person, therefore, ipso facto, I must be having a nightmare. Time to wake up.

Fortunately, I've got a checklist for that.

I was just about to try number four (without a bed) when Uncle Dale interrupted.

"Relax, kid, this ain't a dream! It's all real! Just look!"

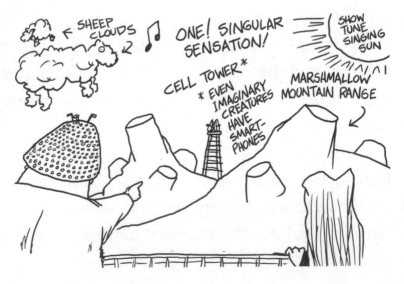

Meanwhile, Cole got right to work.

"After deft evasion of the bounty huntress Loraine," he said to his viewerless live stream, "we boarded an air-bound vessel toward our next destination, which is . . ."

Cole looked up.

"Why, the Bermuda Triangle, of course!" cried Gumdrop.

"The Bermuda what?!" I shouted.

"Triangle!" shouted Phil. "Though it kinda looks more like a lazy drawing of Texas."

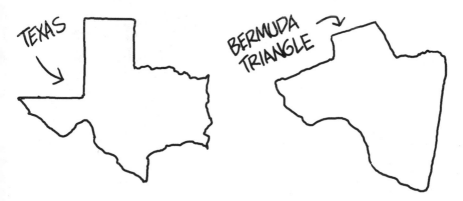

I shook my head. "Now what?"

"That's where we'll meet Grumpus, the portal master, and get some answers to this whole imagination migration situation," added Gumdrop.

"Whoa, Grumpus," said Dale. "Is he still running that fantasy way station?"

Phil said, "Yup. Ever since he came over during the Great Mythical Migration of '59."

Dale turned to me. "How about that, Bobbie? We're going to meet the actual Grumpus!"

Their mouths moved. Words came out. But I had no idea what they were talking about.

Gumdrop sensed my confusion. "Bobbie, dearest, this situation with imaginary creatures crossing the boundary into the real world is quite the conundrum."

I looked up "conundrum" on my phone.

I wasn't buying it.

I said, "I don't get it. That boring Topher/Bigfoot dude and the unicorn sparkle brigade all seem pretty harmless to me."

"Not all imaginary creatures are harmless," said Phil.

"There are many unsavory ones. Imagine if vampires, werewolves, laser ghosts, and swamp minions all crossed over. Madness! Sheer madness!"

Okay, so the thought of living with a werewolf does seem kind of terrifying.

"I still don't understand why I NEED TO BE HERE!" I shouted.

"I want to be here," interrupted Cole. "I can help. Let me help!"

"What the #$%!! is THAT?" I cried.

Everyone turned and looked to the horizon.

This woman does not give up.

"We're doomed!" Gumdrop yelped.

"Evasive maneuvers!" Phil commanded.

"This is gonna be awesome!" Cole yelled.

"Do I look fat in this spaghetti strainer?" asked Uncle Dale.

Chapter 19

Great. My uncle has a crush on a bounty hunter—which sounds like a cheesy romantic comedy you'd see for ninety-nine cents.

Before I could slap some sense into Uncle Dale, Phil placed a large bazooka thingy in my hands.

Phil said, "When she gets close, fire at will!"

That's pretty high up on my list of worst things you can hear in a hot-air balloon.

STUFF YOU NEVER WANT TO HEAR IN A HOT-AIR BALLOON

1. WE'RE LOSING AIR!
2. WHEN SHE GETS CLOSE, FIRE AT WILL!
3. I SHOULDN'T HAVE HAD LIVER-AND-BEAN CASSEROLE FOR LUNCH!
4. PASS THE LIGHTER FLUID, IT'S HIBACHI TIME!
5. DO YOU MIND IF I PRACTICE MY BAGPIPES?

I stared at the bizarre weapon. "What does this even do?"

"Sprinkle cannon! To intercept her Frozen Marshmallow Missiles!" Phil said without cracking a smile.

Of course . . . what else would it be?

As Loraine drew closer I could see the anger in her eyes; she wasn't used to losing and she wasn't about to start now.

YOU MESSED WITH THE WRONG BOUNTY HUNTER!

MARSHMALLOW GUN

POOF! POOF! POOF!

POOF! POOF!

"Fire, Bobbie!" Gumdrop shouted.

"Great shot, Bobbie!" shouted Cole. "The sprinkles are destroying the marshmallows!"

Okay, I'm not going to try to explain how marshmallows can shoot down a balloon or how sprinkles can take out marshmallows. You're just going to have to go with me here. In the Trans-Dimensional World, weird stuff happens.

Unfortunately, the sprinkles didn't slow Loraine down. They only made her angrier. She swooped in closer!

Loraine cried, "Set the balloon down NOW! Before I shoot it down!"

Uncle Dale was smitten. "Awesome pterodactyl. Jurassic period. Vintage."

I turned to the elves. "Maybe we should listen to her?"

Phil: "No way!"

Loraine circled around for another strike. I steadied my sprinkle cannon for the inevitable marshmallow onslaught when I was suddenly met with Cole's phone shoved in my face region.

"It's Bobbie Mendoza, former savior of Christmas, hero of the Trans-Dimensional realm, currently under fire from an unhinged bounty hunter! Any thoughts, Bobbie?!"

"Irritation!" I shouted.

"Earlier today I have you on record saying you were normal and 'not weird,' but this appears to be the exact opposite of normal. How do you respond?"

I WANT TO GO HOME!!

"Fire, Bobbie! Now! Now! Now!" shouted Gumdrop.

But it was too late. Cole's stupid questions had distracted me from Loraine's attack.

Hello. What's the number one thing you don't want to hear on a hot-air balloon?

Gumdrop screamed, "We're losing AIRRRRRR!"

Yep. We were. And fast!

"We're going down! Brace for impact!" shouted Phil.

We were falling, out of control. Headed toward what I could only assume was a pit of hot chocolate lava or a nest of children-eating dragon-bears.

This was it. The end. Reluctant heroine eaten by weird, mutant bears.

"We're going to CRASH!" yelled Uncle Dale.

≋ thump ≋

"Wait. What?" I said.

"We landed softly. We didn't crash!" cried Cole.

WE'RE ALIVE!

"But where are we?" asked Phil.

"Sounds like the ocean?" said Uncle Dale.

"OH dear!" said Phil. "I think . . . we may have landed on . . ."

MERMAID ISLAND!

Whaaaaaaat?!

"Mermaid Island is the most wondrous place in the entire Trans-Dimensional universe!" explained Uncle Dale. "It's like Hawaii meets Switzerland meets Narnia . . . but with MERMAIDS!"

"This just gets better and better!" cried Cole.

"They say the second you lay eyes on a mermaid you fall in love for the rest of your life," said Phil.

That's when things got really strange.

Glenn?

Chapter 20

Turns out we'd landed on Mer-*man* Island. Big difference.

Mermaids are exactly how they've been portrayed in movies and TV. According to Gumdrop and Phil, they have long silky hair that never gets tangled despite living in saltwater. They have flawless skin that never needs sunscreen. And, of course, they have the voices of angels that are always singing original songs about the majesty of the ocean.

A mer-man, however, is . . . well, he's a lot like Glenn!

Phil, Gumdrop, and Uncle Dale were more than a little disappointed.

Phil said, "Um, Glenn, maybe you could just point us in the direction of Mermaid Island."

"Happy to walk!" added Gumdrop.

"Chillax, bros," said Glenn as he pointed to the sky. "You're still wanted by that angry lady. I can help! And hey! I made fish tacos!"

We all looked up. Loraine and her pterodactyl were closing in fast. There really wasn't time to argue. We tumbled out of the balloon basket and followed Glenn to a large sand dune.

"In here!" he shouted.

"That's a sand dune," I pointed out.

"Nah, it's an optical illusion created by the Mirage 3000! Check it out!" he shouted as he rode his Segway into the dune like he was riding through a waterfall.

"Where'd he go?!" I shouted.

"C'mon, Bobbie, more adventure awaits!" said Cole, as he followed Glenn into the sand.

First a locker. Now a sand dune. Following this kid was getting old fast.

Chapter 21

The sand dune led to a large cave that smelled vaguely of salt water and Axe Body Spray.

"What is this place?" I asked. "Are we safe here? Where is Loraine? And most important, where are those fish tacos?"

"Take a chill pill, little lady, you're totes safe! This is the mer-cave and these are my mer-bros!" Glenn said.

Four tank-top clad mer-bros turned from playing *Grand Theft Jet Ski* to check us out.

It was a Dude Cave. The kind of place my dad would have liked to hang out in while my mom was shopping.

"Whoa, whoa, whoa, is that Bobbie Mendoza, savior of Christmas and all-around groovy preteen chica?" said Trevyn—the tannest of the bunch.

"How do you know who I am?"

"You and your uncle are leh-gen-dary!" cheered Kevin—who had the spikiest hair of the bunch.

"We are?" I said.

"We are!" Uncle Dale said.

I tried to roll my eyes, but I found that for a brief moment, the eye-rolling command in my brain had been replaced by the dreaded "blush" feature.

"Not that I care or anything . . . but why'd you rescue us?" I asked.

"Because of the Imagination Wars of course!" Juan Carlos Jimenez said.

"Whoa, whoa, whoa—I think the word 'war' might be a little intense, bro!" said Glenn. "It's more like an Imagination Scuffle. But you're here to fix all that, right?"

I looked over to Gumdrop and Phil. I could tell from the looks on their faces that once again they hadn't told me the whole truth.

"I thought I was here because of my cheer," I said.

"Yes, err . . . cheer is a nice thing, but uh . . . yes, we're in a bit of a bind when it comes to the imagination area . . . ," said Gumdrop.

"Yes, and hopefully you can help us figure it out!" said Phil.

"So you lied to me again!" I shouted.

"No, we didn't lie! I mean, not exactly," interrupted Gumdrop. "You see, Bobbie, we just didn't tell you every bit of the truth because we felt you'd, you know, ignore us."

Never.

Trust.

Elves.

It was time for the full story.

"Wait, wait, wait!" I interrupted. "So you want me to talk to this Grumpus guy?"

Gumdrop smiled and sat next to me. "That's where you're mistaken, Bobbie; this Grumpus guy . . . he wants to talk to you!"

Chapter 22

Am I famous?!

Perhaps being the only human child to have crossed over into the Trans-Dimensional World twice can do that for you. What's it like being a celebrity?

A girl can dream.

But apparently this Grumpus guy is a big deal and he asked specifically for me. He'd heard what I did with the whole Christmas thing and wanted to see if I could help him fix this portal problem.

"Okay, so how do we get to him?" I asked. "Our hot-air balloon is busted and, according to that security camera, there's a very angry Loraine storming around outside your super-secret hidden mer-man cave."

WHERE'D THOSE IDIOTS GO?!

"Glad you asked, little lady," said Glenn. "To get to Grumpus and the Bermuda Triangle, you'll need to take the Trans-Dimensional subway!"

"A Trans-Dimensional subway!" said Cole with far too much enthusiasm.

"Yep, and it stops right here. A train will arrive in the morning."

"We have to stay here? With you guys? All night?" I asked.

"A sleepover!" yelled Glenn.

"Awesome!" agreed Trevyn.

"We'll make s'mores!" added Juan Carlos Jimenez.

"Terrific," I said as non-terrifically as I could.

Meanwhile, Cole went into full hyper-geek-drive.

It was going to be a long night.

Chapter 23

I lay awake for a long time. I went over and over my situation in my head. Why did this Grumpus guy really need me? Why is it they always pick the person who wants nothing more than to hide in plain sight to be the person with a neon sign over her head saying . . .

I don't want to be special. I just want to be me. As in no big deal. Just another girl who likes waffle-pops and painting her toenails black.

"Because you are a big deal," a voice said.

"Who said that?" I asked.

"I did," said the voice.

It was dark. The voice sounded familiar.

I sat up. I looked around. "Where are you?" I said.

The voice said, "Nowhere. Everywhere. Right next to you. Far, far away."

I looked around the mer-men cave. I could see the shapes of sleeping figures. Next to me was Uncle Dale snoring loudly. I shoved him.

"Uncle Dale, wake up!" I whispered.

He didn't budge.

"He can't hear you," said the voice.

"Why not?" I demanded.

"Because he's not there."

"Wait. What? He's right there. I can see him. He's . . ."

"Wait for it."

"I'm dreaming," I said.

"Bingo."

"That means you're not real."

"Oh, I'm very, very real."

"You can't be real if I'm dreaming."

The voice chuckled. "If I'm not real . . .

Then I woke up.

"No. I mean, yes. I mean . . ."

"A nightmare?" asked Cole.

"I'm fine," I said.

"I used to have nightmares a lot. Mostly about

getting bad grades," said Cole. "My mom said it's because I'm an overachiever."

His mom sounds smart. But I didn't want to talk to Cole about my squid nightmare.

"What are you still doing up?" I asked him.

"Thinking," Cole said. "Something doesn't quite add up about this whole mission."

"What do you mean?" I asked.

"Well, it seems strange that Grumpus would want to talk to a human."

"*That's* the strange part?" I asked.

"Just promise me you'll be careful tomorrow," Cole said.

"Yeah . . . as careful as I can be," I added.

"You sure you don't want to talk about your bad dream?" he said.

"Trust me, I'm good," I said.

But I didn't feel good. Not that I've been counting, but that was the third time in a row I had the same nightmare.

And each time it's felt more and more real. I mean, I know bad dreams can be caused by stress—and I guess almost being shot down by a crazed woman on a pterodactyl is stressful—but this felt different.

Should I do what Cole said and talk to someone about it? Or maybe I could just try and think more positive thoughts? Maybe I could binge watch cute-kittens-chasing-laser-pointers videos before bed?

Who knows? But one thing was for certain, I was definitely not going back to sleep that night.

Chapter 24

Morning came, and I spent a lot of time pinching myself and looking behind me. But no squid appeared.

I was awake. I think. I'll get back to you.

After breakfast burritos, we finally left for the Trans-Dimensional subway station.

This part finally made some sense to me. I rode the New York City subway once with my dad when I was eight, and I felt like everyone on board was some sort of weird, magical creature.

BEARD GUY

BAG LADY

SAXOPHONE DUDE

3 CELL PHONE GUY

"But wait!" I shouted. "Why didn't we just take this convenient little subway when we jumped through my locker? Why the superdangerous hot-air balloon?"

"Because in the balloon you wouldn't need to disguise yourself," said Phil.

Disguise myself?

"You're almost certain to have made Loraine's NICE List by now, so we're going to have to make sure you don't look like . . . you know . . . you."

We were going undercover! Hopefully I'd get to wear a cool costume!

Maybe I'll be a hippogriff with a Fu Manchu, or maybe like a half porcupine/half eagle that also shoots lava out of her eyes.

But before I could brainstorm any more great ideas

that involved me looking super awesome, I saw Gumdrop open his phone and scan me with it.

"What are you doing?" I asked.

"I'm scanning you with the Trans-Dimensional
transformation app. It's going to assess your body
mass and give us the quickest and easiest transformation," said Gumdrop.

BEEP BEEP. The device was done.

"Looks like the kid's a troll," Phil said.

Wait. What?! I was going to be a . . .

BOBBIE

TROLL BOBBIE

TROLL HAIR

TROLL NOSE

WEIRD TROLL SUSPENDERS

Chapter 25

So Cole and I transformed into trolls.

But Uncle Dale was way too big to be a troll so he had to disguise himself as something else.

DOES MY BUTT LOOK BIG IN THIS?

Honestly it was a lot like riding a regular subway—but instead of smelling like wet trash and pee, it smelled more like gasoline and burning hair . . . probably because there was a dragon with the sniffles sitting a few rows down.

After brief stops at the Pegasus Palisades and Cyclops City to pick up some passengers, we pulled into the central terminal of the Trans-Dimensional metropolis otherwise known as the Bermuda Triangle.

We exited the subway car under strict instructions from Gumdrop and Phil to remain quiet so as not to give away our identities.

It's a good thing I was speechless. Seeing a *T. rex* arguing with a giant tree monster over his coffee order will do that to you.

We walked for what felt like miles through the mazelike hallways of the Bermuda Triangle subway station with each new turn revealing one bizarre Imaginary Creature after another.

There was some sort of Hippo-Lobster that was quietly shining the shoes of the Easter Bunny. There was a giant centipede getting a manicure from a very overworked Fairy Godmother. But most intriguing was a large and looming store called NIGHTMARES

'R' US that sat completely empty—almost abandoned.

"Whoa! What's in there?!" shouted Cole.

"Shhh!" said Gumdrop. "Keep your voices down."

"What's in there?" whispered Cole.

"It's a store where all the creepy-crawly things shop," said Phil. "You know, a vampire can get some coffin accessories or a vegan zombie could find some tofu brains."

"Why is it empty?" he asked.

"It's been out of business ever since the subway line stopped running to Nightmare Island," added Gumdrop.

Nightmare Island?

I had lots of questions about what sort of terrifying things could live there, but before I could ask any I saw something truly scary.

"Oh dear," said Gumdrop. "It appears as though Loraine and her overlords at SCUD have placed you at the very top of their NICE List!"

I had four questions.

1. HOW LONG HAD THESE POSTERS BEEN UP?
2. WHY WAS I THE ONLY ONE ON THE POSTER?
3. WHERE DID THEY FIND SUCH AN AWFUL PICTURE?
4. IS THAT A GO-GURT STAIN ON MY SHIRT?

But of course I got no answers because something even weirder happened. My eyes in the picture started moving. I got closer.

"Bobbie, get away from there!" whisper-shouted Phil.

Then something even weirder happened.

I started talking to myself. Or more like yelling.

Oh no, there must have been some sort of security camera in there. Alarms blared. Lights flashed!

We'd been spotted!

Phil grabbed me. "We gotta run!"

We only made it a few feet when suddenly a spotlight hit us from above, and we heard a familiar, furious voice over a loudspeaker.

"Don't move a muscle!"

"Can I blink?" asked Cole. "That uses muscles. I have to blink. I have dry eyes. If I don't blink—"

I hissed. "Shut up!"

It was Loraine. She must have tracked us down. I guess that is a pretty valued skill on a bounty hunter's résumé.

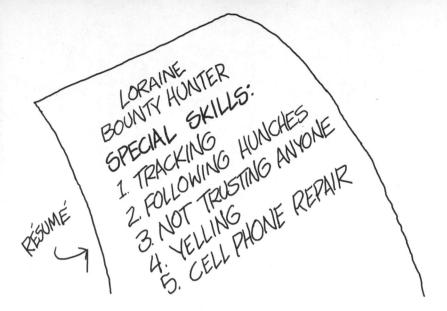

LORAINE
BOUNTY HUNTER
SPECIAL SKILLS:
1. TRACKING
2. FOLLOWING HUNCHES
3. NOT TRUSTING ANYONE
4. YELLING
5. CELL PHONE REPAIR

RÉSUMÉ →

Suddenly, I felt my head squirm and squiggle, as I noticed my troll disguise seemed to be melting off me like hot wax.

We were caught! "What now?" I yelled over to Phil and Gumdrop.

"Not quite sure. Grumpus just told us to meet him at the train station," said Phil.

"Someone should teach this Grumpus guy to be more specific," said Cole.

For once I agreed with him, but that's when I saw it. I could barely make it out through the haze of the harsh spotlight, but as I squinted I saw a flashing neon sign.

All it said was . . .

Huh? But what other choice did I have?

"Follow my lead," I whispered through gritted teeth.

I slowly shuffled to my left, as the gang followed me.

"I said don't move!" yelled Loraine.

She was marching toward us—the spotlight casting her with a sinister halo.

I looked ahead. The neon sign had changed.

Hold on?

That's when the floor opened beneath us.

TRAP-
DOOR →

Chapter 26

I love slides. (I'm a kid, after all.) However, there is one type of slide I don't like: a surprise slide accompanied by two humans and two elves.

We tumbled down a dark and winding chute for what felt like hours but was probably only a few seconds. Luckily, we landed gracefully at the bottom.

NOT SO GRACEFULLY

We looked around. There was a door just ahead. We slowly made our way over. We opened the door and looked out.

It was a massive, cavernous space that almost felt like the inside of an old church except that instead of pews and stained glass there were hundreds of ancient-looking TV monitors with fuzzy black-and-white images and a spiderweb of metallic tubes that zigzagged all over the place.

And right at the center of it all was the man/creature/gnome we'd all been looking for. . . .

EXCELLENT! MY GUESTS HAVE ARRIVED!

Grumpus continued, "So wonderful to see you! I am Grumpus: Master of Portals!"

"You sent me the message?" I asked.

"I did," he replied. "I'm glad you noticed. Sorry to not welcome you more properly."

I had so many questions, but before I could ask, Cole stepped forward and held up his phone to live-stream.

"Hello there, Grumpus, the name's Cole Crusterman, reporter with the *Barking Beagle*, thank you for having me! So what is this wonderful space we're in?"

"Ah, Cole! I do love inquisitive, young minds! Yes indeed, Cole Crusterman, this is my portal way station, where the glorious wonders of children's imaginations are filtered, collected, and organized by yours truly."

"Fascinating. So if a child dreams about . . . a break-dancing kitten, it's your job to make sure that kitten has a home in the Trans-Dimensional World?" asked Cole.

"A break-dancing kitten . . . why, if I'm not mistaken, that's something you imagined a few years ago. . . . I thought I recognized you, Cole! Yes! And if you'd like to check in on Sir Meows-A-Lot I can pull him up right here!"

Grumpus typed Cole's name into the computer and the words "break-dancing kitten."

"It's just how I imagined him."

"Of course it is!" said Grumpus.

Cole continued, "And how did you get into this line of work?"

What was Cole up to?

Grumpus went on, "Another wonderful question, Cole! Many, many years ago I accidentally found my way to the OTHER side of the Trans-Dimensional portal, where I was placed as a garden gnome in the backyard of a wondrous family of eight STU-PENDOUS CHILDREN! And while I was in their company I marveled at the glories of a child's imag-ination. The wonders that they created in their backyard were truly astounding. When my time in the service of the family came to an end, I returned here, where I created a safe home for children's dreams."

"What about nightmares?" Cole asked.

"What about them?" said Grumpus.

"We just saw the trains to Nightmare Island are no longer running. . . ."

"Yes," Grumpus said. "Very observant, Cole! Now if I could talk to Bobbie for a quick moment."

Cole nodded, still trying to process things as Grumpus focused his attention on me.

Grumpus whispered, "Bobbie, you and I are quite similar."

"We are?" I said.

"Yes," said Grumpus. "We've both had fascinating experiences on the 'wrong' side of the boundary. Which is why I need your help! There's a portal on Mermaid Island that I think is the cause of the issue."

"Mermaid Island," shouted Gumdrop and Phil at the same time.

Grumpus smiled. "Exactly! And I'd love to send you and your wondrous team there to locate the troublesome portal and report back to me as to why it's open and if possible—close it down."

"Wait, that's it? I hope you don't mind me asking, Mr. Grumpus . . . but why can't you do that yourself?" I asked.

"Of course I don't mind you asking, Bobbie! I love

how curious your mind is! The reason I can't is simple . . . if there's a leak in your sink you don't call a
trapeze artist, you call a plumber, right?"

"Huh?"

Chapter 27

Plumbers? Trapeze artists? Cole was right. Something didn't quite add up here.

Before I could ask any more questions, Grumpus slid over to a large computer bay and began typing—his chubby fingers moved like hummingbird wings.

A small blurry dot of light started to appear in the middle of the room. It slowly expanded into a large rectangle. It looked like a door, a door of light.

No way, José.

I stuttered, "D-Dad always said don't jump into portals on an empty stomach!"

I began to sweat. My heart raced.

As I stared into the swirling portal to Mermaid Island, I had an odd sensation. Like when you think something's wrong, but you don't know why? Mom gets it all the time. I call it Mom-sense.

Cole and I couldn't be the only ones to feel it. Uncle Dale? The elves? They had to feel it too.

I guess not.

Grumpus smiled a toothy grin. "Come now, Bobbie and Cole! I can't keep this portal open forever!"

I don't know if what I did next was based on curiosity or fear, but before Grumpus could move, I rushed over to the computer and typed in "BOBBIE MENDOZA."

What in the world? Suddenly, Grumpus grabbed Cole and me by the arms and flung us closer to the portal.

"What is it you really want from her?" shouted Cole.

"I want for you to be very scared," Grumpus said.

"Huh?"

Grumpus yanked a lever next to his computer and that's when both Cole and I went flying.

Chapter 28

Darkness.

Cold.

Stench.

Super stench. But not like bad cheese or a fart marinating in a hot car on a summer's day while you stared out the window and pretended it wasn't you.

No, not like that. It smelled like FEAR. Like a bad dream. Like a nightmare! But I wasn't asleep, right?

I heard a deep, guttural growl and turned to see . . .

My brain hadn't caught up to my eyes just yet. If it had it would've started Bobbie's Emergency Fear and Survival Protocol.

BOBBIE'S EMERGENCY FEAR AND SURVIVAL PROTOCOL

1. SCREAM
2. PEE PANTS
3. SCREAM AGAIN
4. PEE PANTS AGAIN
5. CURL UP IN A LITTLE WET BALL AND HOPE IT ALL GOES AWAY

I hadn't fully processed what I was seeing when someone grabbed me from behind!

Obviously, I kept my cool.

Sort of.

It was Uncle Dale with the elves and Cole. He muffled my scream until I could breathe.

"This isn't Mermaid Island, is it?" I whisper-shouted.

"What was your first clue?" asked Gumdrop.

"That no-good dirty gnome," echoed Phil.

"So what do we do now?!" I asked.

"Hide," said Phil.

We ran! The sound of hooves and claws and blood-curdling screams followed us through hazy mist.

But there was no escape.

Just like it says on the postcard.

Before I could ponder the horrifying ways this horde of nightmare creatures was going to torture us . . .

. . . we hit a dead end.

This was it. We turned around to face the mob of monsters. I was scared. Terrified.

A particular nasty-looking zombie in serious need of dental care stepped forward. "Which one of you is the special one? Which one of you is Bobbie?!"

What?! No! Not the *special* thing again! I'm sick and tired of . . .

What? NOOOOOO!

Before I could say anything, they grabbed him. As I reached to stop them we were all interrupted by a horrible . . .

SCREECH

We all looked up.

RAKKKK

It was Loraine! We were all saved!

Not all of us.

Chapter 29

I'm in a meadow. A soft, green dream meadow. And there's beautiful music playing, like the kind of pleasant dream jazz that you hear in the dream organic grocery store or in a superspiffy dream elevator that's taking you to a dream room full of fluffy dream couches and free dream dessert. And it's warm. Beautiful and warm.

Dreamy!

But wait a second. A black smudge appears out of the corner of my eye. Where have I seen it before? I turn to look, but it's gone.

Uh-oh.

Now the smudge is bigger. And it's in the other side of my eye. Not again.

Wait. Why is it suddenly so cold? And the soft music and warm colors are now warbling together into an ugly, off-pitched shriek that sounds like when our neighbor's teenage son tried to start a rage-polka band called the Dead Accordions.

My legs feel tingly and tight. I can't breathe. And that's when I see it.

Again.

This is one persistent giant dream squid. Persistent and growing. His squid tentacles looked like they'd been drinking protein shakes and lifting weights since the last dream.

I'm completely wrapped up in a tentacle death grip. Squeezing. Squeezing. I can hardly breathe when I hear a familiar scream . . .

There's nothing I can do. The tentacles squeeze tighter and tighter. My field of vision grows narrower and narrower. I take one last gasp and . . .

I caught my breath and swallowed hard. "Yeah. A nightmare. And Cole was in it too."

I looked around. "Cole! We left him behind! He's still on Nightmare Island!"

"We'll get him back," said Uncle Dale. "Don't worry."

But I was worried. This dream felt even more real than the last one. What was wrong with me?

And Cole! He'd sacrificed himself for me!

"We have to go back. We have to rescue Cole!" I shouted.

Phil tried to calm me down. "Easy, Bobbie. We all want to do that, but before we can rescue Cole we have to get out of this cell."

"Cell?" I said.

That's when I first noticed we were in a jail cell.

"What's going on?! Where are we?" I asked.

"No idea," said Phil. "Loraine dumped us in here."

"She is rather perturbed with us," said Gumdrop.

"I don't know why," said Uncle Dale. "It's all Grumpus's fault. His portal machine sent us to the wrong spot."

Or did it?

"No. I think Grumpus sent us there on purpose," I said.

"Why would he do that?" asked Uncle Dale.

"I don't know," I said. "But those Nightmare Island freaks were sure hot to get their hands on me. Like, how did they knew who I was?"

"You think Grumpus set this whole thing up?" asked Phil.

"Again. Why?" asked Uncle Dale.

I didn't know. But I was sure going to find out. Just as soon as we got out of this locked cell and figured out where we were and how to get to where we needed to be and what we were going to do when we got there.

That's a lot of unknown unknowns. I don't know about you, but when I face a lot of unknown unknowns I start to freak out. I start to hyperventilate.

I start to panic.

Uncle Dale looked me square in the eye. "Everything is going to be okay."

I breathed. Sometimes Uncle Dale can be convincing. And as silly as it sounded, at that moment I really just needed for someone to tell me everything was going to be okay.

"Trial?" I asked.

"Is it me?" Uncle Dale whispered. "Or did Loraine change her hair?"

No one said anything.

"Maybe it's just me," said Uncle Dale.

Chapter 30

With our hands bound, Loraine marched us down a long, dimly lit hallway. What did she mean it was time to stand trial? Were we going to a courtroom with a judge and a jury? I hoped it wouldn't be like that terrible TV show that Uncle Dale likes to watch at two in the morning . . .

We boarded an elevator and

WE'RE BACK WITH MINOR CRIMES, MAJOR PUNISHMENT. THE DEFENDANT IS CHARGED WITH FARTING AND BLAMING IT ON AN INVISIBLE DOG!

LOCK HIM UP!

Loraine pressed the button for the ground floor.

"Where are you taking us?" I asked.

"Quiet!" she grumbled.

The elevator was shiny and gold plated, full of mirrors, and near the buttons there were dozens of bizarre-looking advertisements.

Great. What crazy part of the Trans-Dimensional World were we in now? Were the elevator doors going to open to a litter of lava-drooling gerbils?! Or perhaps a school full of prepubescent wizards riding around on old mops?

"Please, Loraine, we think something fishy is going on with Grumpus," Uncle Dale pleaded.

"Yeah!" I added. "Cole is trapped on Nightmare Island and we need to go rescue him!"

"Save it for the tribunal," she said.

Tribunal??? What in the heck is a tribunal?!

The doors to the elevator opened and we were met with a very strange, yet somewhat normal sight.

"Wait a minute . . . where are we?" I whispered to Gumdrop.

"Oh dear . . . it would appear as though we're being taken to the monthly meeting spot of the Security Council of United Dimensions," he said.

"Which is located in . . . ?"

"The one place in the whole world where humans and Trans-Dimensional Beings can share the same space without one noticing the other," Phil said.

Gumdrop pointed out a window. "Vegas, baby!"

"Vegas?" I gasped.

"Hurry now!" said Loraine. "They're waiting for you."

Chapter 31

What I witnessed walking into conference room 4B in the Bellagio hotel in Las Vegas was perhaps the strangest sight I'd ever seen in the real world since I watched my dad try yoga for the first time.

Seated at a long, elevated table were what I guessed to be all the representatives of SCUD. It was either that or the Trans-Dimensional All-Freak Volleyball Team.

From the far left we had . . . a pumped-up Easter Hare (not a bunny ANYMORE), some guy with weird hair and sunglasses they referred to as the King, Cyril the Nearsighted Cyclops, Nessie the Loch Ness Creature (monster is no longer politically correct), Vlad the Vegan Vampire (only drinks the blood of Vegans), Abraham Lincoln (don't ask), some sort of alien named Xalkathuru (pronounced Richard), and a very normal-looking woman with glasses named Karen. She spoke first.

"We're the representatives of the Security Council of United Dimensions—an organization designed to safeguard and protect the boundaries between the human world and the Trans-Dimensional World. We hereby recognize Loraine the Bounty Hunter—and an enforcer of the NICE List—Loraine, you have the floor."

Loraine cleared her throat. "Thank you, Karen of Fresno. And thank you, all distinguished members of this council."

"Karen of Fresno?" I said out loud.

"Silence!" shouted Loraine. "Now, this council created the NICE List to protect both sides of the boundary from Inter-Dimensional Invaders."

They all nodded together in agreement as Loraine continued, "That is why I have brought to you these 'boundary hoppers.' Defendants one and two, Philip K. Sugarloaf and Gumdrop Q. Schmelzer, did willingly cross the boundary in an attempt to lure defendants three and four, Bobbie and Dale Mendoza, to the Trans-Dimensional side."

"I'd like to add that I didn't really want to go in the first place!" I shouted out.

"Zip it!" growled Loraine. "Now, in the initial boundary breach, defendants one and two allowed an entire herd of unicorns and one fun-sized unicorn into a human middle school."

There was an audible gasp followed by a hushed whispering among members of the tribunal.

"Thankfully, yours truly captured them and stored

them alongside several other nefarious creatures inside my Shrinkifier Medallion for safekeeping," boasted Loraine.

Loraine went on, "On the Imaginary side of the boundary, all four defendants did willingly attempt to evade capture and in so doing endangered the sanctity of the Trans-Dimensional Barrier as well as the lives and sanity of all creatures on both sides."

"Is this true?" asked the Easter Hare.

"Therefore," she went on, "I recommend the council votes unanimously to wipe all Trans-Dimensional memories from the minds of the two humans."

Wipe our memories?!

"And for the elves, an immediate sentence to a life of cleaning toilets at the Sasquatch train terminal of the Bermuda Triangle," said Loraine.

"Hold on," I shouted. "A memory wipe? So Uncle Dale and I would have our memory wiped clean of this whole thing?"

"Yes," said Loraine. "As well as your memory of saving Christmas and all of Dale's past adventures as well."

"So I can go back to being normal?" I asked.

"Bobbie, don't do it," said Uncle Dale.

But I'd heard enough. "Wipe my memory now. I agree. Do it, Loraine."

Uncle Dale looked disappointed. Phil and Gumdrop huddled together in shock as Loraine pulled out a thick metallic rod with a glowing orb on the edge.

"Does the council authorize a memory wipe of a one Bobbie Mendoza?" said Loraine.

They all nodded their heads.

Uncle Dale shouted with panic in his voice, "Don't do this, Bobbie! Your memories make you who you are. Don't erase a part of you!"

But I'd already made up my mind.

Loraine took a few steps closer to me, powering up the device.

"Now look directly at me," she said.

"Please, Bobbie!" cried Uncle Dale.

LOOK DIRECTLY INTO THE LIGHT. NO SUDDEN MOVES.

And for a split second I allowed myself a blissful moment where I imagined I didn't have these insane memories. A moment where I was normal. A moment where elves didn't break into my locker to lure me into magical adventures. A moment where my uncle didn't write ten-thousand-word articles on how there was a national toilet paper shortage because mummies were coming to life. And finally, a moment where an annoying but incredibly brave kid named Cole didn't sacrifice himself for us. . . .

It was nice. Boring but nice.

Because like I said, I'd already made up my mind.

Loraine grinned. "Smile for the camera, sweetie."

I smiled.

Then I snatched.

I spiked the necklace on the ground and watched in what felt like slow motion as it broke into a million tiny pieces.

And just like I hoped, the room burst into chaos.

Chapter 32

There was that unicorn smell again. But this time it was worse. WAY worse. It smelled like pancake batter and liquefied anchovies that'd been sitting out in the sun for a few days. I guess being shrinkified and trapped inside a locket with a sweaty Bigfoot, a herd of unicorns, and whole bunch of other nasty creatures can really make the BO worse.

But enough about the smell, I needed to get to my first order of business.

RUNNNNNNN

The room was rapidly filling up with all the crazy creatures now let loose from Loraine's locket. There was of course the unicorn herd, a terrified-looking Bigfoot I assumed to be Topher, a litter of dragon-cubs, a very old werewolf who used a walker with tennis balls on the end, and a horrifying host of ghosts that shot lasers from their eyes.

As the insanity unfolded, I grabbed Uncle Dale, Phil, and Gumdrop and sprinted toward the exit.

SHUFFLE SHUFFLE

"Stop them! They're getting away!" cried Loraine.

We rushed out of the room, into a long carpeted hallway.

Ugh! That's always the problem with a perfectly executed plan: you need to have a follow-up plan.

"In here!" Gumdrop shouted, pointing toward the Librarian Association meeting that was happening in room 4A next door.

"Librarians?!" I said.

"Just be very, very quiet, and I bet we can blend in," said Phil.

There were no other options. We quietly tiptoed inside only to see something far more bizarre.

Before we could process the idea of a Librarian Fight Club, the door behind us burst open and Loraine, flanked by several angry members of SCUD, barged inside. "There they are!"

That's when over a thousand members of the Librarian Association turned toward Loraine and—in perfect unison—raised their index fingers to their pursed lips and let loose the most powerful *shushing* I've ever witnessed.

We had to get out of there! But the only way out was *in*! So as the boxing match began, we pushed and shoved our way through the conference room toward an unmarked exit.

We burst through the door to the sight of cooks, waiters, and fry chefs barking orders in a variety of languages. I looked over my shoulder—had Loraine followed us?!

"This way!" yelled Uncle Dale from around a corner.

He must have found the exit!

Nope.

Before I could dump the hot pot of curry all over Uncle Dale's head, I spotted one of the waiters headed for the main floor of the casino!

We pried Uncle Dale away from his curry and escaped to the packed casino. We had to hurry. Loraine couldn't be far behind.

"This way!" Phil shouted as he pointed to another exit.

We ran but were quickly cut off.

We turned and ran.

Straight into Loraine, Abraham Lincoln, and her goon squad of nightmare freaks.

Loraine smiled. "There's no way out."

"But there is a way up," shouted Uncle Dale.

"What?" I cried.

Uncle Dale yanked me and the elves toward an open elevator. Somehow the doors closed on Loraine in the nick of time.

We began traveling upward. Smooth jazz played over the speakers . . . and over Loraine's slowly softening rage-fueled screams.

I caught my breath, only to look to my left and see a very confused couple in a tuxedo and white wedding dress.

Chapter 33

What now? The hotel was only thirty-three stories high and we were nearing the top floor! I was out of brilliant ideas. That's when Uncle Dale said something insane.

Uncle Dale has a history of shouting random words that really don't make any sense.

But this time it made sense. He was pointing to an advertisement on the elevator walls. "There's a zip line on top of this roof," he said. "It'll take us to the next building!"

"But I'm afraid of heights!" shouted Phil.

"And I'm afraid of zip lines!" shouted Gumdrop.

"And I'm afraid of dying while falling from a zip line!" I shouted.

"Well, if anyone has a better plan I'm very open to hearing it because—"

DING!

The elevator doors opened to the roof of the building. We peered out. The zip line was a few hundred yards to our left. Loraine and her SCUD goons were nowhere to be seen. The coast was clear.

"RUN!" yelled Uncle Dale.

We ran! And within a few steps I knew this zip line plan wasn't going to work. Partly because of the large sign that read . . .

And . . . that's when the door to the stairwell burst open.

Once again we were trapped. Except for real this time. Let's summarize the facts.

To my left, a broken zip line and a two-thousand-foot drop, and to my right, Loraine at rage level ten billion.

There was nothing else to do except surrender. Or I could try wetting the bed again, but I was pretty certain this wasn't a bad dream.

Per usual, Uncle Dale took a different approach.

"Um, Loraine," croaked Dale. "I know this might not be the best time, but when this is all over—what do you think the chances are for a guy like me and a bounty hunter like you . . ."

I wanted to roll my eyes, but for a brief moment I was sort of kind of moved by Uncle Dale's last shot at lunatic love. We were on the rooftop of a scenic hotel, surrounded by insane mythical creatures and—almost as if it were on cue—beautiful music started playing and then . . .

RUMMMBLE

What was going on? Was this another dream? There was music. There was a rumble. There was Abe Lincoln. There were . . .

MERMAIDS!

Say what? I looked down and rising from an open portal in the swirling pool below was a very bizarre sight.

Nope. Not a dream. Even I couldn't make something up that bizarre.

The warrior mermaids were rising from a portal in the fountain below. They looked like Navy SEALs except with better hair and, you know, mermaid tails. I was just about to ask about their hair conditioner when . . .

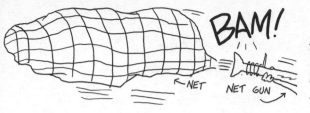

BAM!

← NET   NET GUN ↗

Loraine shot us with her net gun! We were trapped!

"Grab the prisoners and take cover!" yelled Loraine.

Loraine dragged us like a sack of fish toward her as the Flying Mermaid Warriors prepared to attack.

"I'm gonna take that as a maybe on the whole date thing!" shouted Uncle Dale.

Suddenly, a large trident PINGED into the ground, severing the thick ropes of our net in half!

We were free! The mermaids were rescuing us?!

I looked up and a particularly fierce and majestic mermaid looked me directly in the eyes. "Come with me if you want to save Cole!"

To be honest, I probably would have come with her if she'd said pretty much anything.

COME WITH ME IF YOU WANT TO SEE TOILETS MADE OUT OF PUDDING.

SURE. WHATEVER.

165

It was a rescue! I grabbed Uncle Dale, Phil, and Gumdrop, and we ran for the ledge.

"What are we doing?!" shouted Phil.

I said, "We're jumping."

"No. No jumping," said Gumdrop.

"I weigh about two hundred seventy-five," said Dale. "Those mermaids are like a buck twenty. No way they're catching me."

"You're two hundred seventy-five?" laughed Phil. "You're at least three and a quarter. You know, you're only lying to yourself."

"This spaghetti strainer adds ten pounds easy. Naked, I'm two hundred seventy-five."

"Naked?" cried Gumdrop. "How am I going to get that image out of my head?"

Idiots. I was surrounded by idiots. We were being chased by Abe Lincoln and a sack full of unicorns and these morons were worried about Jet Pack Amazon Mermaids' upper body strength. I'd had enough.

WE'RE JUMPING!!

166

"I guess we're jumping, then," said Phil.

"Apparently," agreed Gumdrop.

Dale said, "I really am two hundred seventy-five."

"NOW!" I screamed as Loraine and her goons ran toward us.

We were flying! I looked up to see Loraine rushing to the edge of the building, furiously attempting to get us back with her net gun! But it was no use. We were out of range.

I wanted to say something snappy to her as we escaped. Something like, "Sorry, Loraine, gotta jet!" or maybe, "You'll *net-er* catch us now," but before I could identify the perfect quip Uncle Dale interrupted me!

"Loraine, watch out!" he yelled.

In the insanity of the mermaid jet pack rooftop scuffle, the unicorns got loose. Again. And one of them immediately took a bead on Loraine's butt.

This was a big one. Not the little fun-sized guy I rode through my locker. It was lights out for Loraine. Unicorn coma city. Unfortunately for Loraine, she was poked unconscious on the ledge of a thirty-three-story building.

As we flew down toward the majestic fountain and entered the swirling portal, I leaned back and asked my mermaid rescuer, "Where are we going?"

"We're taking you home," said the mermaid.

Chapter 34

Mermaid Island was not at all like the slow-motion shampoo commercial that Phil and Gumdrop expected. It was more of an off-the-grid military base full of high-tech surveillance gear and of course— mermaids. Lots and lots of mermaids.

I THOUGHT IT WOULD SMELL MORE LIKE COCONUTS.

MERMAID ISLAND

We were quickly ushered inside for questioning and separated from the loudly snoring Loraine.

"Hey! Where are you taking her?" said Uncle Dale.

"She took a heavy dose of unicorn toxin," said the mermaid named Katy. "We just want to make sure she wakes up calm."

I don't think Loraine has ever been calm, awake or asleep.

They seated us in a cold, dark room with a table, a few chairs, and a one-way mirror that I assume hid a bunch of other mermaids on the other side. I could tell Uncle Dale was worried.

"Please let me know when she wakes up," said Uncle Dale.

A voice over the loudspeaker said, "Please be seated."

Uncle Dale quietly sat as a door opened. The mermaid that caught me when I jumped off the roof entered. She held a thick stack of official-looking documents in one hand and a cup of coffee in the other.

"All right there! The name's Tabitha—leader of the mer-woman brigade," she said.

"Sorry to pipe in," Phil said. "But is this the real Mermaid Island?"

"This here is Mer-woman Island. I'm afraid what you're thinking of is just a myth."

"No coconut bras?" said Phil.

"No coconut bras," said Tabitha.

"Um . . . thanks for the dramatic rescue back there," I said.

"Don't mention it. And the funny-looking one . . . ," she said, pointing to Uncle Dale. "That was real brave what you did catching the angry helmet lady."

Uncle Dale blushed. "I hope she noticed."

"So why rescue us?" I asked.

"We've been monitoring your progress since you hopped the boundary. When you contacted our fellow species mates on Mer-man Island we paid much closer attention."

"About that . . . so the mer-men and the mermaids

don't really hang out together much?" I asked.

Tabitha sighed. "It's mer-WOMEN! Do I look like someone's maid?!"

"No," I gulped. "I just . . ."

Tabitha calmly interjected. "We're just independent gals over here. Plus, the guys really like fish tacos and hair gel, and we're more into protein shakes and leave-in conditioner. Makes more sense for us to have our own islands. Still, we have mixers."

MER-MEN ← ← OPPOSITE SIDES OF THE DANCE FLOOR → MER-WOMEN →

"So if you've been monitoring us, then you must know what's going on with Grumpus," I said.

"Know?! We've been trying to bring it to SCUD for months, but they won't listen. The portal glitches, the boundary hopping . . . it all leads back to him somehow."

"Why won't they listen?" asked Gumdrop.

"Because Grumpus holds a lot of power."

"What's his plan?" Uncle Dale asked.

"We think it might have something to do with Nightmare Island," she said. "But we're not sure what your pal Cole has to do with it."

"No, that's the thing!" I said. "They really want me. Cole sacrificed himself for me."

"Mmph, you humans are braver than I thought," said Tabitha.

"And what about elves?" said Gumdrop.

"Your mettle has yet to be tested," she said. "But you are rather adorable."

Gumdrop blushed. "You're actually not so bad yourself."

What was going on here?!

Before I could ask that, we heard a loud voice over the intercom . . .

Chapter 35

Loraine was fuming when we approached her holding cell.

"I'm gonna report all of you to SCUD," shouted Loraine.

"You most certainly won't be doing that, Loraine," said Tabitha.

"Oh yeah, and why not, Sgt. Fishy?!"

"Because these humans are critical to helping you resolve your NICE List once and for all."

"Calm down!" said Tabitha.

"No way! You kidnapped me! You're all traitors! When I get outta here I'm gonna . . ."

I'd had enough.

It worked. See, I have skills.

"We are not traitors," I said. "In fact, my uncle Dale saved your life. You were about to fall thirty-three stories and become a Viking pancake when he risked his own life to save you. And maybe if you stopped always yelling like a crazy person and accusing everyone around you of Trans-Dimensional treason you might be able to see that."

Maybe it was my tone, maybe it was the fact that I was shaking, but Loraine got real quiet. She looked over to Uncle Dale.

"You saved me?" she asked him.

"Yes, ma'am. Happy to do so," he said with as much charm as a grown man with a spaghetti strainer on his head can manage.

Loraine squinted at him real hard, as if she were trying to see if he was telling the truth or maybe trying to crack an invisible walnut with her eyelids. I guess Uncle Dale passed the squint test because after a few moments Loraine's face softened and she said something I didn't expect.

"Thank you very much. That's very brave."

"My pleasure," said Dale.

Were we about to witness the lighter side of Loraine?

Guess not.

"Listen, Grumpus and a bunch of nightmare creatures have kidnapped our friend Cole and we need to rescue him," I shouted.

"Prove it, pip-squeak!"

"I can't! Unless there happen to be security cameras on Nightmare Island," I said.

"There aren't!" shouted Loraine.

"I was being sarcastic!" I yelled.

"Wait a minute," said Gumdrop. "Cole's live stream!"

Of course! That was brilliant! Cole had practically been live streaming everything to an audience of zero. We could be his first viewers. I mean if he hadn't been partially digested by a dragon-bear by now!

"You want proof," I said. "I'll get you proof. But first . . . can we borrow a cell phone?"

Chapter 36

Chapter 37

So Grumpus was trying to get my squid nightmare? Is that why he sent us to Nightmare Island? And what machine was he going to hook Cole up to?

But before I could ask any of these questions, I noticed Loraine's nostrils had flared to the size of grapes. Those big fat ones that cost seventy-nine cents each at Whole Foods.

Gumdrop said, "As you can see, Grumpus is up to something rather devious and/or nefarious."

"He means 'bad,'" I said.

"But where could they be?" asked Phil. "They're

not on Nightmare Island anymore."

With a few keystrokes, Tabitha projected a screen grab of Cole's live stream onto a larger video screen.

"Enhance!" she said.

"Enhance," she yelled again.

The letters got clearer. I could see it was a window . . . and the letters S, U, and R were clear.

"Sur?" said Phil.

"No, no. It's backward. So it'd be 'RUS'!"

Then it hit me!

"No!" I shouted. "It's 'R' US. Cole is in NIGHT-MARES 'R' US! The store that was closed down in the Bermuda Triangle train station."

"That must be Grumpus's evil lair," said Uncle Dale.

"Well, what are we waiting for . . . ?"

We all turned around to see Loraine, calm, cool, and collected. Though her nostrils were now the size of coconuts ($29.99 at Whole Foods).

"Loraine! You're on our side now!" said Uncle Dale.

"Let's roll!" she commanded.

And roll we did.

Chapter 38

We needed an elaborate rescue plan! Luckily, I'm great with plans!

BOBBIE'S ELABORATE RESCUE PLAN

1. SNEAK INTO BERMUDA TRIANGLE TRAIN STATION
2. RESCUE COLE FROM NIGHTMARES 'Я' US
3. DEFEAT GRUMPUS
4. SAVE THE WORLD
5. EPIC PARADE/CELEBRATION

I had to scratch out number five. Remember, when you're the "chosen one" and you save the world, you have to keep it to yourself. I modified my list.

BOBBIE'S SLIGHTLY MORE REALISTIC RESCUE PLAN
(NOW WITH ADVERBS)

1. STEATHILY SNEAK INTO BERMUDA TRIANGLE TRAIN STATION
2. COURAGEOUSLY RESCUE COLE FROM NIGHTMARES 'Я'US
3. HEROICALLY DEFEAT GRUMPUS
4. EPICALLY SAVE THE WORLD
5. AWESOMELY EAT WAFFLE-POPS ALONE IN MY ROOM

We didn't have disguises, which meant we couldn't take the subway line. So the mer-women airlifted us.

As we were getting ready to leave, Loraine approached me. "Your uncle really saved me?" she asked.

"He did," I said.

"You know, I'm not the type of gal that usually needs saving."

"I figured."

"You seem like you don't need much saving either."

"I don't know about that. I get scared all the time."

Loraine chuckled. "Fear . . . it ain't about fear. I'm terrified a lot in my line of work."

"You are?"

"Going toe-to-toe with a dragon-bear that wants to eat your spleen for brunch is enough to make anyone scared."

"Do you ever get, um . . . nightmares?" I asked.

"Used to . . . ," she said. "But I got over that."

"What changed?"

"I learned you just gotta embrace your fears."

"Embrace? Like . . . actually hug them?"

Loraine chuckled.

"No, not like actually hug them. If I hugged a dragon-bear, I doubt it'd go well."

THIS IS NICE, BUT I STILL HAVE TO EAT YOU.

YEAH, I KNOW.

Loraine continued, "More like . . . run toward it. Don't run away from it. And if all else fails, imagine your fear in its underwear."

"Really?" I asked.

"That was a joke," laughed Loraine. "C'mon, kid, I can make jokes."

"Let's move," barked Tabitha.

And before I knew it, I was strapped onto the front of a large mer-woman wearing a jet pack. Loraine was next, but she shook her head.

"I've got my own mode of transportation," she said.

Chapter 39

We soared through the thick, sugary clouds of Candy Land and over the large grassy fields of Ninja Puppy Island (which has secret portals located in the back of every washer/dryer in the world).

As we neared the Bermuda Triangle train station, I sensed a change in the air. Maybe I was coming down from the sugar high of sticking my tongue out during a particularly fluffy cotton candy cloud, or we were getting close to Grumpus and his ghoulish goons.

I caught the glint of the train station in the distance when suddenly my eyes focused on something strange on the horizon. I squinted. I couldn't quite make out what it was, but it looked like a large white sheet. Kind of like a piece of paper. But this white piece of paper had arms and legs.

I cried, "What on earth is that?"

"No idea," Tabitha yelled over the roar of her jet pack.

We'd find out soon enough. It was moving straight toward us.

We were almost to the train station when I noticed writing on top of the page. It was a name. A name I recognized.

"Okay, seriously, what is that?" shouted Tabitha.

Wait! Of course! It was Cole's nightmare!

For sure an A minus was what he feared the most. Somehow Grumpus must have made it come to life. But before I could tell everyone, Loraine screamed, "Evasive maneuvers!"

Ugh. Why are maneuvers always "evasive"? Why can't it be "casual maneuvers" or "lackadaisical maneuvers," or maybe even "I'll-get-to-it-eventually maneuvers"?

We were under attack! The flying mer-women scattered as they avoided getting swatted down by the college-ruled King Kong.

"AHHHHH!" I screamed as Tabitha dodged a fatal swipe that sent us clumsily jostling through the air.

"We're too heavy!" she yelled.

Was she saying I was fat? I mean, I know waffle-pops aren't exactly the healthiest of foods, but now wasn't the time.

Tabitha shouted, "Sorry, kid, but I gotta drop you off early!"

She started to unhook me.

"Wait! What?" I cried.

We swooped close to the ground and suddenly I was weightless, then falling, faster and faster toward the ground.

Good thing I stuck the landing.

Gracefully.

I dusted myself off and looked up. I was alone now. Above me, an aerial dog fight between the flying mer-women and a giant A minus was waging. I looked down. The train station was eerily quiet. What gives? I wondered.

That's when I saw it right in front of me.

And inside I could hear a familiar sound.

AYEEEEEEE COUGH COUGH EE

It was Cole screaming.

Chapter 40

I snuck in through the back entrance of the store, creeping past a supply of gross products, like vampire dental floss, aged toilet paper (single ply, for mummy wrapping), and something called Zombie Lipless Gloss?

I quietly peered out to see Cole— strapped down on a table, with some sort of bizarre vac- uum cleaner device

stuck to the top of his head. It looked like he was sleeping.

A vampire next to him said, "Technically, boss, an A minus isn't really that bad."

A werewolf added, "C's get degrees!"

Grumpus stomped his tiny foot. "I don't need a lecture in academia! Where's the girl?! Her nightmare is the one we felt across dimensions. She's the one we need!"

So he did want my squid nightmare! But why? What was Grumpus up to? Before I could figure it out, Cole started to stir.

"The boy is waking up. What should we do now, boss?" said the vampire.

A mummy entered. "I can really try and scare him good this time!"

"Oh please, no one's afraid of a mummy," said the vampire. "You're just a wad of toilet paper with legs!"

"Well, you're just an old guy with weird dietary restrictions!" protested the mummy.

"Stop making fun of my peanut allergy!" yelled the vampire.

Grumpus fumed. "Prepare a portal! We're sending him back to Nightmare Island, where he can learn to fear much more than just a bad grade."

"Again, I don't think an A minus is technically a bad grade," said the clueless vampire.

198

Grumpus yelled, "Get some glue in the supply closet and stick it back on!"

I was in the supply closet! They were walking toward me! I needed a new hiding spot and fast!

I snuck into the nightmare bathroom (which was surprisingly clean) without anyone noticing me. But now I had to come up with a plan to save Cole! They were going to send him back to Nightmare Island for good! What could I do? I looked at myself in the mirror.

I looked at my reflection and thought . . . why me? Why does everyone think I'm so special? I get zits, my hair is too flat most days, and just the thought of talking to my mom about boys makes my armpits sweat. I mean, I'm normal!

So why won't anyone let me act like it?

Why am I stuck in a werewolf bathroom in the Bermuda Triangle as an evil gnome tries to steal my nightmare and ban Cole to Nightmare Island?

I started this day just wanting to be invisible. Or at least hoping to blend in.

I was tired of looking at my reflection. I took a step away from the mirror when I noticed something. Toilet paper stuck to my shoe. Great.

Because now I had an idea . . .

What happened next definitely wasn't my best idea, but it wasn't my worst idea either. It was probably my best worst idea or my worst best idea.

It was my only idea.

Chapter 41

As I tiptoed out of the werewolf bathroom in my toilet paper prom dress, I heard Cole shouting for help.

I waddled as fast as I could in the direction of Cole, when suddenly I heard a voice ahead. It was Grumpus. He was talking to someone in hushed, angry tones.

Curiosity overcame me. I had to see.

SOON YOU'LL GET A TASTE OF YOUR OWN MEDICINE! SOON YOU WON'T HAUNT ME AGAIN!

Who was he talking to? What was in that jar? He must have sensed someone was watching him because suddenly he turned around and glared at me.

I was caught!

Grumpus stared at me. "What are you doing, corpse! Go help the others!"

He bought my disguise! I mumbled a quick apology and shuffled after the sound of Cole's screams.

I found Cole strapped to a chair in a room off the hallway. The nightmare creatures were setting up the portal.

The vampire protested, "Hey, none of us are ghouls."

"I dated a ghoul once," said the werewolf. "She was nice."

"What does 'grisly' even mean?" asked the vampire.

"To cause horror or disgust!" shouted Cole.

"Aww, thank you," said the werewolf. "That's very sweet of you."

"It's a shame we gotta send this kid away; I'm learning a lot from him," said the vampire as he powered up the portal.

"Hold on!" I shouted. They all turned to look at me.

Great. My mouth had moved before my brain had time to catch up.

They were all staring at me. I had to improvise. C'mon, Bobbie, think!

"Grumpus . . . uhh . . . well . . . he bought everyone pizza!" I said.

Oh no! There's no way anyone would buy that.

Wow, undead people really are kind of stupid. I guess I just needed to roll with this.

I approached Cole and the others. "He said he's sorry for being mean earlier, and for me to take care of Cole while you guys chow down."

The werewolf pointed to the zombie. "Did he remember to get a side of gluten-free brains for Rick?"

"He sure did!" I said. "Now run along, the pizza's gettin' cold!"

They all excitedly rushed out of the room. Stupid nightmare creatures.

I quickly started to untie Cole.

"Shhh, Cole, it's me, Bobbie," I whispered. "I'm here to rescue you."

Cole whispered back, "Oh, Bobbie! Thank heavens, but wait . . . there's no pizza?"

I was a little disappointed too. But there was no time . . . we had to get out of there before they realized it was all a ruse. I had finally got Cole freed when I slowly felt myself spinning.

Oh no. It was the toilet paper . . . my mummy wrapping!

"I thought there was something fishy here," said the real mummy as he pulled the toilet paper toward him like a wind-up toy.

HEY! THIS IS TWO PLY! ALL MUMMY WRAPPINGS ARE ONE PLY!

"Run!!!" I shouted.

Cole ran toward the exit. I tried to follow but the two-ply was surprisingly durable. Grumpus and his goons drew me closer, peeling me out of my disguise like an undead onion.

"The boy is getting away!" cried the werewolf.

"Let him go; this is the human we need," said Grumpus with a sinister glare.

Chapter 42

I must have been asleep. But I didn't feel like I was asleep.

I was in a white-walled room, sitting at a table by myself in front of a large jar. A dark, sinister light pulsated from within. What on earth could be in there? That's when a door opened and Grumpus entered.

I tried to say, "What're you up to, you no-good dirty gnome?!"

But what came out of my mouth was a tad different.

I guess I was dreaming. But what was Grumpus doing here?

"You're wondering why I'm here inside your sub-conscious?" he asked.

"Ain't no party like a pizza . . ." I stopped myself. Clearly, he was the one in control.

He took a deep breath, like he was about to begin a long speech.

"Bobbie, I'm in search of the perfect nightmare. A nightmare birthed out of stress, anxiety, and of course *fear*. A nightmare even more powerful than my own. A nightmare so powerful it could only come from someone—like me—who's experienced both dimensions; who's seen both the horrors of the real and imaginary world. The only other human I know to have done that is your uncle Dale, and you can imagine how lame his nightmares are."

UNCLE DALE NIGHTMARES

Grumpus was right about that.

Grumpus went on, "You and I aren't so different. We both experienced things we can't talk about. Things no one would believe. Things that if we spoke of them, people would think we were crazy. As I told you before, I was once a simple gnome who found his way to the wrong side of the Trans-Dimensional Border."

He continued to monologue, "When I felt your nightmare, I could tell it was a tense, vivid, palpable dream from across the Trans-Dimensional Barrier. I had to know what it was. So, I used my powers of deception to lure you here. Then I sent you to Nightmare Island with the hope of whipping your basest fears into a frenzy—but alas the human boy and the bounty hunter ruined those plans."

Get on with it, I thought. Is it possible to fall asleep inside your own dream?

"But you returned to me," said Grumpus. "A very

brave girl you are! And I'm here to help you, Bobbie. I want to free you of your fear. Whatever it is that haunts you in your dreams, give it to me."

He pointed to the jar on the desk. "I can place it in here, where it won't bother you ever again."

The idea was tempting. But what was Grumpus going to do with my nightmare? Whatever it was, I couldn't trust him.

I shook my head defiantly.

Grumpus smiled. "Very well, then. . . . I'll take it from you forcefully!"

Suddenly, the room went black. I couldn't see anything and I started feeling dizzy. The room was spinning. I saw flashes.

Oh no. I could feel it coming on. And I could hear Grumpus's voice . . .

I couldn't breathe!

I jolted awake!

GAHHHHHHHH!!

"Where am I?! What just happened?!" I yelled.

"You were under Grumpus's dream device. He must have taken your nightmare like he did mine," said Cole.

"But why? And where is he taking it?" I asked.

Loraine was one step ahead of us, typing rapidly on one of Grumpus's computers.

"That Grump!" she shouted. "He's accessing a portal into the human world."

"Which portal?" I asked.

"Apparently one that had been left open earlier today," she said.

"My school locker?" I asked.

Phil turned to Gumdrop. "It was your day to close the portal!"

Gumdrop threw his hands up. "No! It was your day!"

"We have to go NOW, Bobbie! Who knows what Grumpus has planned?" said Cole.

But I knew. And before we went back to school I had to grab one thing.

Chapter 43

We rushed toward the glowing portal in pursuit of Grumpus. Who knew how long he'd been on the other side? We were running out of time!

I had no idea what would happen next, but I did know one thing: I was not gonna let Cole jump in first this time.

Okay, so I don't know who invented magical portals, but I do have a few suggestions for improvement.

Magic *still* has its limitations. I could barely breathe, mostly because I could feel (and smell) two tiny elf butts jammed against my face inside my locker!

I finally opened my locker from the inside, and we all tumbled out into a heap on the school floor. I looked up—it was only two thirty. School was still in session.

I forgot how slowly time moved in the real world compared to the Trans-Dimensional World.

"Where is he? Where's Grumpus?!" shouted Loraine.

This was strange. It was eerily quiet and the hallways were empty. No one was in class. What was going on?

And that's when it hit me. I knew where Grumpus was!

THE PEP RALLY!

Chapter 44

All this time messing with mermaids and zombies has been less than a day in the real world. That meant that when we got back there was a huge pep rally scheduled in the gym that day. That had to be where Grumpus was headed with my squid nightmare!

We all ran toward the gymnasium. I could sense a dark and creepy vibe clouding the school. It felt just like one of my nightmares, except this time I was awake!

And I wasn't the only one to notice it.

"Something feels amiss," yelled Gumdrop.

"'Amiss' means weird or funky," added Phil.

"Yeah! What's going on, Bobbie?" shouted Uncle Dale.

"I think Grumpus stole my nightmare and he's going to do something really amiss with it at the assembly!" I yelled.

"How dastardly!" shouted Gumdrop.

"Totally messed up," added Phil.

"Wait. What's your nightmare?" Loraine asked.

"Ms. Mendoza!" a deep voice interrupted.

"No! He's not my nightmare!" I cried.

Uncle Dale looked confused. "Seems pretty nightmarish to me."

"Who are these strange people?!" demanded Mr. Lindenberger.

For a second I thought about trying to explain,

but before I could even try, Mr. Lindenberger's eyes widened. Then his hands began to tremble as they dramatically rose and pointed to something in the distance.

"The . . . the horror! The horror!" he shouted.

I turned around to see . . .

"Farting spider!" said Gumdrop. "My worst nightmare!"

Yup. We were going to be late to the assembly.

Chapter 45

If there's one positive thing about hanging around with a Trans-Dimensional bounty hunter, it's that if you're ever challenged to a fight by a bunch of super evil nightmare creatures from another dimension, she'll have your back.

The werewolf attacked first. Like a lupine lizard, he leapt off the wall and lunged at us. It was fast, but Loraine was faster!

Loraine's net ensnared the snapping, hissing wolfman in a neat little bow! Score one for Loraine! But a split second later the vampire was on her—fangs bared like a rabid dog.

Loraine dodged a fatal bite when Uncle Dale jumped in!

The vampire melted before Uncle Dale's garlic/curry gasp.

Loraine cried, "Nice move, Metal Head!" as she

netted the vampire.

Uncle Dale blushed. "Thanks."

The mummy charged Phil and Gumdrop, but the elves were too quick as they grabbed separate ends of the creature's body wrapping.

"PULL!" yelled Phil.

Gross. Just gross.

Meanwhile, Cole was "battling" the spider.

Cole turned to me. "I told you I'm a proud member of Arachnids Are Awesome! This guy is a sweetheart."

Cole is so weird.

There was just the zombie left. I guess it was going to be me versus, you know, it.

"Let's do this!" I shouted.

Huh?

The zombie continued. "I've been living a lie my whole death. I play the part of a zombie to fit in, but I really want to be a jazz dancer or play the accordion."

Sure. Whatever.

I watched as Loraine and Uncle Dale dealt with the werewolf and vampire. Cole had the playful spider in stitches. And Gumdrop and Phil were wrapping up some unfinished business with the mummy.

Good friends. Good times. Weird times. But good times.

But instead of counseling a zombie in an identity crisis, I realized I had to go deal with the scariest monster of them all.

Chapter 46

I rushed into the school gymnasium expecting to find Grumpus implanting my squid nightmare into the brains of all the kids in the school, but what I found was much more horrifying.

EVERY student in the school was laughing at me. It was my worst nightmare. My armpits started to sweat. My tongue dried up. My vision warbled and warped. I went full woozy. This was worse than the dream. This was real! I saw an empty jar roll out from the stands and hit my foot. I looked down and read . . .

BOBBIE'S NIGHTMARE

UH-OH.

228

I looked up. That's when I saw it. And it saw me.

"Hello, Bobbie," said a familiar evil voice. "We meet again."

It was Grumpus standing on stage grinning from ear to ear. Everyone in the auditorium froze—as if someone had pushed pause on a movie.

Grumpus pointed to my laughing squid nightmare. "There it is, Bobbie . . . your waking nightmare. Awake in the *real* world!"

I couldn't breathe.

Grumpus monologued, "You've fallen right into my trap. You've helped me fuel the fire of fear. Petrifying, immobilizing fear! Fear that is the opposite of imagination. Fear for those children who tormented me so many years ago. Those children who used their imaginations to send me to space or throw me like a football or ride me atop their dog like a tiny cowboy! Those brats will know fear! Now that your nightmare is made real I can enslave the imagination of children once and for all! Now they will feel fear. FEAR OF ME!"

He was right. The fear was real. I was beyond terrified. The fear was about to wrap its dark black tentacles around my throat and squeeze.

But what Grumpus didn't know was that two could play at that game. Everyone has a nightmare. Grumpus kept his in a jar.

And I had the jar.

Chapter 47

I released Grumpus's nightmare. The nightmare boy exploded from the jar and grew and grew into a towering terror. I could see the fear in Grumpus's eyes as—for the first time maybe in his entire life—he was speechless. Though he did gurgle a little bit.

I'd bought myself some time, but that still didn't change the fact that my squid nightmare monster was going to strangle me and then infect the dreams of all the kids at my school.

"HELP!" I yelled as its slithery tentacles wrapped their way around me.

Finally, Loraine, Cole, Uncle Dale, Phil, and Gumdrop rushed into the auditorium.

"Loraine! Help!" I shouted.

Loraine immediately went into action mode, whipping out her exploding net gun and taking aim at Mr. Nightmare Squid.

She fired. But the net just went right through the squid like it wasn't even there. The squid just laughed. What was happening?

Uncle Dale shouted, "It's from your imagination,

Bobbie. Only you can control it!"

WELL, THAT SURE IS CONVENIENT!

Meanwhile, Grumpus was weeping loudly as the evil torturer child slowly strapped him to the rocket.

That's when I noticed that with each scream and wail, Grumpus's nightmare grew bigger. I looked to my squid. Same deal. Were they feeding off our fear? Was Uncle Dale right? Was I somehow in control here? I didn't feel in control.

I felt helpless.

Loraine noticed too. She yelled across the gym, "Embrace your fear, Bobbie!"

The squid lifted me up and drew me close. Whew! Squid breath!

I cried, "Dude, try a mint!"

It drew me closer and closer. I could see my

reflection in its Ginsu-sharp teeth. I had to do something. And I had to do something fast. Embrace my fears? Why not?

I closed my eyes, wrapped my arms around the slimy black squid, and squeezed, trying to imagine it was my old teddy bear (Dr. Fuzzy) or my younger brother, Tad, that one time when he used his monthly allowance money to buy me the new flavor of waffle-pops (crunchtastic cherry).

Time seemed to slow down as I continued to hug the squid.

I had no idea if it was working or not, I just knew at that moment I wasn't being eaten alive in front of the entire school (always a good sign).

That's when I heard Uncle Dale. "Awwww . . . it's so cute!"

Huh? I opened up my eyes and saw that my arms were no longer wrapped around a psychotic demon squid from the deep, but more like a cuddly-wuddly plush toy from the planet Adorable.

It worked!

Loraine said, "By 'embrace' I meant more like a choke hold, but what you did was great too."

Before we could celebrate too long I looked over to see Grumpus sobbing like a baby, as the giant child held a lit match up to the end of the bottle rocket.

There was a time I really wanted to see the evil gnome shot off into space. But now I sensed a panic. A panic I knew all too well. He was scared just like me.

I wanted to help him. And I'm not sure why this came to my mind.

I saw Grumpus close his eyes. And then it happened.

The rocket vanished into thin air and Grumpus collapsed into a grateful heap onto the stage floor.

Uncle Dale smiled at her. "Looks like you can cross off the top name on your NICE List."

Loraine smiled back. "And I owe it all to you."

Uncle Dale blushed as Loraine leaned in and gave him a kiss on the cheek. Uncle Dale swooned.

Then I turned around see over four hundred kids staring at me from the bleachers. Oh yeah, they'd watched the whole thing.

I knew exactly what to do.

I took a bow.

Chapter 48

Loraine, holding a strange device, stepped in front of the stunned student body and cleared her throat. "Okay, kids, everyone look straight ahead. Cole . . . you too."

"Wait, what is that thing?" I asked.

"Memory erasure thingy. We can't have these kids knowing about the Trans-Dimensional World."

"Me too?" asked Cole.

"Afraid so," said Loraine.

He sighed and began walking toward the rest of the kids.

"Wait, Loraine," I said. "Cole's the smartest, weirdest, sometimes annoyingest, and most definitely the bravest kid I ever met. If there's anyone or anything else out there like Grumpus who wants to mess with the border and get on your NICE List, don't you think you want kids like me and Cole around to help?"

Loraine squinted at me, then her face softened. "I suppose I can bend the rules just this once."

Cole beamed. "Thank you, Loraine! You won't regret it!"

"But you can't go around yapping on any live streams or writing any blog dot com stories about this. Gotta keep it to yourself," Loraine warned.

I smiled. "Don't worry, Cole. I know just the place where we can talk about everything."

Chapter 49

So this is my life now. Every Sunday night Cole, Uncle Dale, and I head down to the Nondenominational

Church of Happiness and Stuff for our weekly Trans-Dimensional support group meetings. I used to hate these things, but honestly it helps to talk about stuff. Plus, Cole really seems to love it!

Cole and I are good friends now. I started working with him at the student newspaper and it has really helped me meet a lot of new people. We don't talk about our adventures with unicorns or Segway-riding mer-men or farting spiders when we're at school, but sometimes we'll share a quick look that lets me know someone else out there knows I'm not crazy.

Uncle Dale is doing great too. His blog traffic has more than doubled since our last adventure. Up to 134! He still loves going to the support group, but now he loves it even more because sometimes Loraine will drop by unannounced.

Loraine's career as a Trans-Dimensional bounty hunter has really taken off since she took down Grumpus. She still takes her job of protecting the barrier between real and imaginary worlds VERY seriously, but ever since she and Uncle Dale started dating she's lightened up a bit.

Elf dance parties are the best.

Speaking of elves, Gumdrop and Phil now spend a lot of their off-seasons working as butlers on Mer-Woman Island alongside Tabitha and the rest of the mer-ladies.

And as far as Grumpus goes, he and a few of his more sinister nightmare goons are locked up in the most restrictive prison in the Trans-Dimensional World—located on Ninja Puppy Island.

And as for me, not too much has changed. My mom and dad still get a little too proud of me for doing very basic things.

But I guess I've lightened up a bit. I don't worry so much about every little thing. Because worrying and stress and all that stuff just makes you afraid, and being afraid leads to bad dreams, and as of recently I like my dreams.

Ugh, fine, I guess I'll say it . . . it helps to have people around who understand what you've been through. People you can talk to. People who make you understand that it's okay to be whatever way you are.

For me it was realizing that being special can be normal. Like I said, I haven't changed much. I still like to wear black (it still goes with everything, even me), I still like waffle-pops (frozen is better), and I still sometimes like to paint the toenails of my little brother, Tad, when he falls asleep.

I'm still the same me.

Except I've saved the world twice now.

And that's pretty special, right?

The End

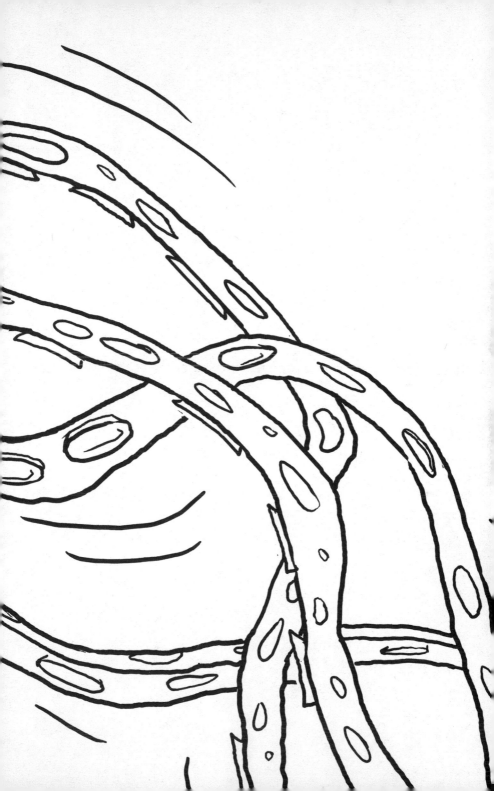

Acknowledgments

We'd like to thank everyone at HarperCollins for letting us go a second round in the ever-expanding Bobbie Mendoza–verse. (Watch out Marvel, farting spiders are the new Thor!) We'd especially like to thank our editor, Nancy Inteli, for championing our silly ideas and our art director, Rick Farley, who really put a lot of thought into how many colors make up a good unicorn tail (seven). And a massive thank-you to our wonderful agent, Dan Lazar, who helped us get *The Naughty List* off the ground and kept pushing for a sequel that finally answers the question—how would a mer-man get around on dry land? It's been a wild ride marked by too much coffee, not enough sleep, and just the right amount of pie.

About the Creators

Bradley Jackson is a screenwriter and novelist living in Los Angeles. His first feature film, *Balls Out*, stars Kate McKinnon, Jake Lacy, Jay Pharoah, and Beck Bennett and was selected as a Critics' Pick by the *New York Times*. He also cocreated the sci-fi comedy series *Crunch Time* for digital behemoth Rooster Teeth as well as cowrote and coproduced the documentary *Dealt,* which won an Audience Award at the 2017 South by Southwest Film Festival and was distributed by IFC/Sundance Selects. This is his second book with Mike Fry.

Michael Fry has been a cartoonist and bestselling writer for over thirty years. He has created or cocreated four internationally syndicated comic strips, including the current *Over the Hedge*, illustrated by T. Lewis, which is featured in newspapers nationwide and was adapted into the DreamWorks Animation hit animated movie of the same name. In addition, he is the author and illustrator of the bestselling middle grade novel series How to Be a Supervillain and The Odd Squad. He lives on a small ranch near Austin, Texas, with his wife, Kim, and a dozen or so unnamed shrub-eating cows.

Also by MICHAEL FRY and BRADLEY JACKSON

"Will keep kids laughing from start to finish."
—*Publishers Weekly*